Dan Latus grew up in Teesside and lives in Northumberland with his wife.

A DEATH AT SOUTH GARE

Private investigator Frank Doy makes an off-duty visit to the South Gare, the breakwater at the mouth of the River Tees, anticipating a spectacular high tide in that wild, windswept place. Instead, he sees a man in the sea with no hope of rescue or survival — and, on the breakwater, three men who may have put him there . . . Frank soon discovers that the man was a greatly-respected local MP. As the only witness to this crime, he himself is now in deep trouble. But he can't just walk away. Though he needs to protect himself, he wants justice for the murdered man . . .

DAN LATUS

A DEATH AT SOUTH GARE

Complete and Unabridged

ULVERSCROFT
Leicester

First published in Great Britain in 2015 by
Robert Hale Limited
London

First Large Print Edition
published 2016
by arrangement with
Robert Hale Limited
London

A catalogue record for this book is available
from the British Library.

ISBN 978–1–4448–2723–1

Published by
F. A. Thorpe (Publishing)
Anstey, Leicestershire

Set by Words & Graphics Ltd.
Anstey, Leicestershire
Printed and bound in Great Britain by
T. J. International Ltd., Padstow, Cornwall

This book is printed on acid-free paper

This one is for John

1

There was only the one vehicle on top of the breakwater at the mouth of the Tees that day. It was a big pickup truck, parked hard against the high steel fence that stopped vehicles going any further. I walked past the truck and down some steps to the next level of the breakwater. Three men were walking towards me from the far end. They didn't look like sea anglers.

They were bunched together and they carried neither rods nor the usual clutter of bags, baskets and bait buckets. Dressed in heavy-duty industrial jackets, trousers and boots, they had their heads ducked down out of the wind and spray until they noticed me. I nodded to the one nearest me as we passed. He blanked me with a hard stare. So did the other two. Tough guys, eh? I thought with a rueful smile. I walked on.

I sensed them stopping and turning round to look after me, but I kept going. They might have a problem, but I certainly didn't. I didn't have a problem in the world. Not that day. Not yet anyway.

Early March. Mid-week, mid-afternoon.

Sunny, but bitterly cold in the strong wind. I was anticipating a raging high tide, a spring tide at that. Earth, sun and moon all in line, and the pull of gravity to match. The prediction for today was 5.9 metres, which would be close to the highest level ever recorded here of 6 metres.

I felt exhilarated as I saw the sheets of spray sweeping through the air at the far end of the South Gare, the big ones reaching up to dash against the lighthouse on the top level. The tumble of huge concrete blocks protecting the end and the sides of the breakwater were doing their best to break up the sea's onslaught, but they were engulfed by a tumult of white water and were scarcely even visible today.

My pace faltered as the sea came foaming over the end and swept along the broad platform of rough concrete towards me. I scrambled a few feet up the sloping wall to get out of the way and took to the narrow ledge that runs round the end of the breakwater, just below the lighthouse. But I didn't go much further. The end of the Gare was out of bounds to sensible people on a day like this.

For a few moments, I stood still and savoured the power and beauty of the sea in all its fury. The roaring and pounding was overwhelming. Clouds of spray swept over me, icy sheets of hissing sea mist that soaked as they touched and made me wince and shut my eyes. I opened them again and prepared to retreat.

That was when I saw a flash of something yellow tossed up in a wave, about ten metres out. I watched and saw it rise to a height and crash back down again, to disappear in the cauldron of foaming, churning sea.

The yellow object reappeared half a minute later. I could see what it was then. For a brief moment that lasted a hundred years I saw that it was a man, a man in a yellow high-visibility jacket, his mouth open as if crying for help or screaming with terror. Then he was gone. I waited, nerves on edge, shocked beyond belief, but I didn't see him again.

There was nothing to be done. Not by me anyway, and not by anybody else in this world. Feeling sick, I worked my way back from my ridiculously exposed vantage point and climbed up to the safety of the top level of the breakwater, just below the lighthouse. Then I stood for a moment and processed what I had seen. A man. No doubt about it. A man beyond help in this life.

The three tough guys who had passed me were gone, as was the vehicle that must have

3

brought them. There was no-one else in sight either when I jogged back.

I guessed I was probably the only person here now. The lighthouse had operated automatically for many years, and there was no longer a coastguard post or a lifeboat at the South Gare. There might have been someone in the old pilot station, I suppose, some sort of volunteer perhaps, but it seemed unlikely. That had been downgraded or abandoned, too. The pilot cutters operated from a base further up the river these days.

I hurried along, although in truth there was no need to hurry. None at all. There was nothing to be done now but pick up the pieces.

Back at the Land Rover, I ducked gratefully out of the wind and started the engine, turning the heater full on. Then I phoned Bill Peart, my detective pal on the Cleveland Force. It wasn't a detective that was needed right now but I couldn't face going through all the hoops you encounter when you phone the emergency number. All that giving of information and personal details first to some civilian support person — who probably doesn't know the location you're talking about, and is just operating from a crib sheet — before you can even get to say why you called.

4

'What can I do for you, Frank?'

'Are you having a good day?'

There was a pause before he said, 'I was. What do you want?'

'I'm at the South Gare.'

'In this weather? You must be mad. You're . . . '

'You're right. I must be. I've just seen a man in the sea, Bill. Off the end.'

'Dead?'

'What do you think on a day like this? Just before I saw him, I passed three hard cases coming away from the end of the breakwater. They were the only people around, and they must have known and seen what had happened. There's even a possibility they put the man there.'

He didn't miss a beat. Probably he was used to stuff like this in his job.

'Stay where you are, Frank. I'll get a car there in a few minutes, and I'll be down myself in fifteen.'

Then he rang off, not troubling to say good-bye, or thank-you for letting me know. None of that civilized stuff that's supposed to make us members of the public feel good about reporting 'incidents' to the police.

So I had to stay here, did I? Shit! I wished I'd waited till I'd got home before phoning him.

5

As it happened, I couldn't have left immediately anyway. When I got out of the vehicle to put my wet gear in the back, I noticed I had a completely flat tyre. Now how had that come about?

Nothing wrong with the tyre, I realized, when I tried to blow it up again. It was just that someone had pulled out the valve and let the air escape. I swore, gritted my teeth and wondered who the hell that could have been.

★   ★   ★

The uniforms arrived first, two of them in a Volvo saloon. They couldn't have been very thrilled about being sent to the South Gare on a day like that, but they were very good about it. Pleasant and respectful, and eager to hear what little I had to tell them. They listened without interrupting. Then they left me sitting in the Land Rover while they drove towards the end of the breakwater, to see if they could see what I'd seen.

Bill Peart wasn't very long after them. By then I'd put in a new valve from the repair kit I carry, got the tyre blown back up and was just putting the pump away. He waved me over and I went to join him in the super-heated atmosphere of his Volvo four-by-four.

'What are you doing here today?' was his opening remark.

'Not much.' I shrugged. 'It was just a spontaneous decision. I remembered there was a high tide today, and came to see how it was getting on.'

'Don't you have enough of the sea at your place?'

'It's different here.'

'Yeah, you're right. It's like being in the middle of the North Sea!'

He shivered and added, 'Are our lads here yet?'

I nodded. 'They drove further on, to see what they can see. Not much, probably.'

'So what did you see?'

'Not much either. Just a brief sighting.'

'You couldn't have been mistaken?'

I shook my head. I knew he had to ask questions like that but I was growing weary of it all already. I was beginning to wish I'd seen nothing at all, or not bothered coming here in the first place.

'Wearing a yellow safety jacket, you said?'

I nodded this time. 'That's what it looked like.'

'Not an angler, then?'

'Well . . . it could have been, I suppose. I don't really know.'

'Did you notice anything else about the

body, apart from the yellow jacket?'

I turned to look directly at him then.

'I saw him trying to scream, Bill. That good enough for you?'

'Jesus, Frank!' he said, shaking his head.

★   ★   ★

We talked a bit more about the weather, the sea and how it was utterly impossible to have done anything about the guy in the water. Even without going to the end of the break-water, Bill knew what it was like along there. So he didn't blame me for not jumping in and trying to perform miracles. Even if I had jumped in, the sea would just have thrown me right back out again. I wouldn't have got anywhere near the man in the water.

Then I told him again about the three tough guys.

'Connected, you think?'

I nodded. 'Like I said, I think they might have put him there.'

'Any evidence?'

'Well, I didn't see them do it, if that's what you mean.'

Bill sighed and said, 'I really wish you hadn't phoned me, Frank. I was having such a good day.'

I ignored that and started up again. I

wasn't prepared to keep all this to myself.

'He could only have been in the water a couple of minutes, at most. And where they were coming from, they must have at least seen him. So even if it was an accident, or a suicide, you would expect them to report it. I take it no-one has?'

Bill shook his head. 'Not yet anyway.'

'Plus, someone took the valve out of my tyre and let it down, which meant there was no possibility of me taking off after them even if I'd wanted to.'

'All circumstantial.'

'All the same . . . '

'All the same,' he agreed.

He asked me about the men. I couldn't tell him a lot. Mid- to late-thirties, perhaps. They wore industrial clothing and boots. And they had looked a mean bunch.

'No safety helmets or hats?'

I shook my head. 'They could have left them in the vehicle.'

'Tell me about that.'

'A big pick-up. Heavy duty. Double cab. American style, but probably Japanese.'

'Colour, make?'

'Silver. Muddy. I didn't notice the make. Maybe a Toyota. That's about it.'

Bill shut his notebook. Then we sat in silence for a minute or two. I was thinking about the poor bastard in the water. I had no idea what Bill was thinking about. Where to get a cup of coffee, probably. We were a long way from a café.

'It's not a lot to go on,' he said eventually.

I agreed.

'Gangland, a vendetta?' he added.

'I don't know, Bill. But pretty bad stuff, whatever it was.'

'Amen to that.'

The uniforms returned soon afterwards. They said they had seen nothing but a lot of sea. I wasn't surprised. If they had been anywhere near the end of the breakwater, they were lucky to have got back again. And the tide still wasn't up to its full height yet.

Bill told them to stay there and keep an eye on the beach until someone was sent to relieve them. Eventually the body would reappear, he said, probably on the beach after the tide turned.

The two constables didn't look thrilled about that but there was nothing else to be done. Bill talked about alerting Search and Rescue and the RNLI as well. That seemed to cheer them up a bit, knowing someone else was going to be involved, but I knew it wasn't going to shorten their vigil.

Turning to me, he said, 'You might as well be on your way, Frank. I'll look in on you, or give you a call, when I have something.'

  'Next year, then?'

  He grinned at last. 'With what you've given me to go on, it might well be next year!'

2

I called to see Jac Picknett before I went home. She had an art gallery in Middlesbrough, and occasionally we did things together. Slept together mostly. We got on fine but neither of us was the committing kind. Maybe we just hadn't met the right person yet. In her case, I was certain of it. She deserved better than me, a lot better.

'Well, look at you!' she said with a particularly lovely smile as I crossed the threshold of her workplace. 'Just as I was thinking no-one ever visits me these days.'

'I came to see your latest exhibition, actually,' I told her. 'What is it this month?'

'This month we feature seascapes by up-and-coming regional painters.'

I shuddered. 'I've seen enough of the sea for one day. Can we go and eat, or have a coffee or something?'

'Ten minutes, Frank. Just give me ten minutes.'

I did. I spent the time not looking at the paintings in the exhibition.

Then we visited an Italian restaurant nearby that seemed to serve as Jac's dining room, she was there so often.

'I'm very busy,' she explained, 'or we could have gone further afield, and then gone on home afterwards.'

I nodded, disappointed to hear we weren't going on home afterwards.

'So what are you busy with?' I asked.

'Our next exhibition. It's not coming together very well, I'm afraid. Artists,' she added with a shrug, 'can be very difficult at times.'

Probably. But there are worse people in the world than artists. I was still thinking of men in industrial boots.

'How about you, Frank? How are you doing?'

I shrugged. 'I need to find another paying client sometime soon, but today that's been the least of my worries.'

I told her about my visit to the South Gare, and the body in the water. She frowned and looked thoughtful.

'Not nice,' she decided. 'Poor man. Who on earth could it have been, I wonder?'

I shook my head. 'They'll find out eventually, but not necessarily soon. Anyway, it will give Bill Peart something to get his teeth into.'

'Oh, yes! Bill. How is he?'

'The same. He doesn't change much.'

Jac smiled, and then laughed. 'Whenever I think of him,' she confessed, 'I see a worried man. Is he always like that?'

'Most of the time. But you should see him when he's just caught a fish. He's a different person then.'

'Hmm,' she mused. 'I'd like to see that. I really would.'

That's what Bill and I did from time to time. Went fishing together. From my place at Risky Point, down the Cleveland coast, it's an easy thing to do.

'I sometimes think the fishing is the only reason he stays in touch with me,' I added.

'Surely not? What about all the cases you solve for him, all those little mysteries where he doesn't make any progress at all until you come along?'

'Sssh! He might hear you. Anyway, this one has nothing to do with me — thank God! I'm not going anywhere near it. He'll have to solve it all by himself.'

Jac laughed. She threw her head back and laughed, laughed enough to make people at other tables smile and glance at me with envy. And make me ache to lean forward and lick her long, smooth, creamy throat.

★   ★   ★

It was late that night when I got back to Risky Point. I climbed out of the car and stopped for a moment to look at the sky. Perfectly clear. No moon, but plenty of starlight. My only neighbour, Jimmy Mack, must have gone to bed. There were no lights on in his cottage, or anywhere else for that matter. The world was at peace. Even the sea was quiet now. Low tide, and all the sea was doing was murmuring somewhere near the foot of the cliffs. A beautiful night. I sighed with contentment and headed for my front door.

As soon as I got inside I saw the flashing light. There were two messages on my phone system. Bill Peart wanted me to call him urgently. I glanced at my watch and decided it could wait. He wouldn't thank me for getting him out of bed in the small hours.

The other message put an end to my contentment. It said, more or less: we know who you are, and what you are; we know you are connected to Cleveland police; we know about Miss Jac Picknett. Our very strong advice to you is to forget everything you saw at the South Gare today. Forget you ever even went there, and get on with the rest of your life.

That was it.

No overt warning about consequences. There was no need. The message was clear,

15

and as clearly understood. There was no danger of me mistaking its meaning.

I thought about it. Somebody had been very busy indeed in the last few hours, checking out who the owner of my car was.

I listened again, and again after that. The voice was middle-class and educated, the accent sort of southern rather than local. The diction was clear. The man was articulate and authoritative. The tone was menacing; the objective clear. The consequences of non-compliance with the suggestion unstated but obvious.

I mulled it over. If they could get what they wanted this way, the easy way, they seemed to be saying, they would accept it and draw a line underneath. Probably they didn't want the fuss that a second murder — this time of a private investigator with personal connections to the police — would inevitably create. But they would, in the end, do whatever was necessary. The choice was mine. It was up to me.

I rang Bill Peart.

'Where the hell have you been?' he demanded angrily.

'Steady on, Bill! I've been getting on with my life, taking Jac out for a meal. You should do that with your wife sometime. It works wonders.'

He grunted. He liked Jac. So I was off the hook.

'Anyway, what was it you wanted to talk to me about?'

'The body.'

'Ah! Before you say anything else, I should tell you I've been warned off talking about it.'

'Oh?'

'There was a message on my phone when I came in twenty minutes ago. I've just been listening to it.'

'What did it say?'

'It's what it didn't say that's worrying.'

I gave him the gist, glad to have a friendly ear to pour it into.

'I'm not surprised,' Bill said with apparent satisfaction when I'd finished my résumé.

'You're not?'

'Not considering who it was that ended up in the sea.'

'So you've found and identified the body?'

He didn't bother answering that question directly.

'James Campbell,' he said after a short pause.

The name seemed familiar, but it was a common enough sort of name. Where had I heard it? One obvious candidate came to mind.

'Not the . . . ?'

'Exactly! The MP.'

Now it was my turn to pause, and to think.

'I'll drop by in the morning,' Bill added. 'Not a word to anyone about this in the meantime, by the way. There's an embargo on it.'

3

She was careful. Always. Something told her she wasn't safe here. Nothing specific, nothing she could identify and point to, but she wasn't at ease. The crowds, these people, this . . .

What she must avoid at all costs was leading them to where she lived. She was still safe there, if nowhere else.

She let the door swing shut behind her and slipped out into the street, to mingle with the common people. Wasn't that what he had called them? She smiled ruefully. He had meant people like her. It was a quaint term, but he had been quite right, as it happened. That's what she was, and all she wanted to be. He was the one with pretensions.

He was also the one with money, of course, and power. So she needed to be careful, especially now she had confronted him. She would. She would be careful. She was under no illusions. There was no love lost between them. Never had been. And now there was money at stake. Big money.

4

The next day started well enough. I got up. I had breakfast and checked the news. No mention of a dead MP having been found anywhere in the United Kingdom. I could have been happy with that if I hadn't had a threatening phone call the night before. As it was, I was in suspense, waiting for something else to happen.

To fill the time, I opened yesterday's mail. Nothing outstanding. So I checked my emails and found one I liked the sound of. Someone representing a major global company contemplating inward investment into the Teesside area would like to speak to me about a job to do with anticipated security issues. The company was called PortPlus. I was invited to phone back. That sounded promising. Checking out their security needs and arrangements was one of the things I did for clients, and right now I was experiencing a fallow period and needed to generate some income.

Before I could do anything about it, though, I heard the sound of a vehicle drawing up outside. A glance through the window told me it was Bill Peart in his big machine. I went out to meet him.

'You're up early, Frank.'

I gave him a stony stare. 'What do you mean? I'm nearly always up by lunch time.'

'To be self-employed, eh? What it must be like.'

He was in a good mood. Top of the world.

'Have you ever thought of trying stand-up?' I asked him.

'Only sometimes, like when the boss wants to see me. Like this morning, actually. He wanted to know what was happening about this dead MP.'

'Already? What did you tell him?'

'What I could. The body had been found and collected. The pathologist would be going to work imminently.'

'That it?'

'More or less. Is that coffee in that pot there?'

I poured him a mug, and another for myself.

'So what did your boss say?'

'He tut-tutted a bit, and told me how important it was to get it sorted urgently. He didn't want the media or the new Police Commissioner on his back all day.'

I could imagine the conversation. Impatience revealing itself already. Chief constables and their senior colleagues are as much politicians as anything else. They have to be, I suppose, but it's amazing how quickly they seem to forget what it's like for the troops out in the field.

What probably made it worse for Bill this time was the fact that the Cleveland Police HQ is only a couple of miles out of Redcar, and hardly any further from the South Gare. So they had a homicide in their own backyard, and it was a tricky one.

'I don't envy you, Bill.'

He smiled. 'Thank you, Frank. That's the nicest thing you've said to me for a long time. Now do you want to hear what we've found so far?'

I nodded.

'James Campbell didn't drown. He was shot dead first, and then chucked in the sea.'

That took me back a bit. 'But I saw . . . '

'I know. You told me. But the pathologist says what you saw was just a freak occurrence. It looked like a cry for help, or whatever, but it couldn't have been. A bullet in the brain had already killed him.'

'And that's certain?'

Bill nodded.

In a way, that let me off the hook. I was almost relieved. There really would have been no point in me jumping in the water yesterday, even if I'd had the inclination.

'Not good, is it?' I said with a grimace.

Bill shook his head. 'It looks like you might have been right about the three tough guys you saw. In fact, it makes me think you were lucky. Instead of letting your tyre down, they could have put a bullet in your head as well.'

That thought had already occurred to me. It wasn't comforting.

'Let me hear that message someone left for you?' Bill suggested.

I played it for him a few times. Each time it sounded just as threatening.

'What do you want to do?' he asked me afterwards.

I shrugged. 'Not much I can do, is there? I'll just carry on as normal. The implied threat to Jac worries me a bit, though.'

'I take it you wouldn't want police protection, or to go to a safe house?'

I just smiled.

'Sure?'

'Especially not now,' I said. 'There's the prospect of a bit of business coming my way.'

I told him about the email.

'Who's it from?'

'Someone working for something called PortPlus. I haven't had time to check them out yet, but some new business would be very welcome. The cupboard's looking a bit bare.'

He nodded. 'Good luck with that.

'Right,' he added, easing himself out of the

23

chair. 'I'd better get on. Let me know if anything else comes in from whoever left that voice message. And my advice is to avoid the South Gare for a little while. Do you want me to talk to Jac, by the way?'

I shook my head. 'I'll have a word with her myself. But she's a busy lady, and I don't want to disrupt her life.'

'Any more than you have already, you mean?'

I wasn't the only one who thought Jac was too good for the likes of me.

★　★　★

I did some Googling about James Campbell after Bill had gone. There was plenty to read. In his short career as a Member of Parliament, the man had made an impact and ruffled an awful lot of feathers. His re-election prospects looked accordingly good.

In a constituency like Redcar, as well as the rest of Teesside, the perennial big issue has always been jobs. No politician has been able to avoid that in my lifetime, or in my father's, for that matter. I suppose all areas that have developed with a high dependency on heavy industry, like steel and chemicals, are like that. So James Campbell had campaigned long and hard about unemployment levels.

24

Surprisingly, the environment also figured prominently on the local political agenda. Perhaps that was because heavy industry does more obvious and visible environmental damage than financial services and banking. So on Teesside there was a sizeable constituency that cared about environmental issues and wanted to repair the damage, and safeguard what was left of the environment. James Campbell was prominent in environmental campaigning.

He was also busy in relation to child poverty, equal opportunities, better housing, improved education, greater life opportunities for young people, care for the elderly and infirm, and more support for those with learning difficulties. In short, I couldn't find anything he didn't support, unless it was tax relief for the super rich. He was impressively progressive. It was difficult to believe a man like him could possibly have any political enemies who were not either oligarchs or simply deranged.

My Googling didn't tell me much I didn't know, although I did now have a better picture of a man in a hurry to get ahead in politics. Even after only three years in Parliament, the call to join the Government front bench couldn't reasonably be delayed much longer.

But that was yesterday — before he got shot.

I found next to nothing about his personal life. In fact, all the press cuttings, talks and PR releases I accessed that first morning seemed to indicate that he didn't have one. In the old days that would have made me wonder about his sexuality. Now it just left me wondering. Perhaps he was simply too busy.

In any case, I reminded myself, it was nothing to do with me. Bill Peart would have to look into that. A simple drowning in high seas might not have merited the expenditure of much in the way of police resources, but the shooting dead of a prominent politician certainly would.

I thought of the threatening phone message, too, and wondered how easy it would be for me to escape the consequences of having visited the South Gare on that fateful afternoon.

5

'You should have been more careful.'

'On a day like that? Nobody there?'

'He was there. The guy. He turned up, didn't he?'

Frustrated, the first man shook his head and sighed. He said nothing more. The silence between them grew.

The man in the suit, the one who was paying the bill, got up and walked over to stare out of the window. He was thinking; it was a mess, a dog's breakfast.

He turned and said, 'We need to keep him quiet.'

'That's easily done,' the other man said with a rough chuckle. 'We don't want witnesses any more than you do. Take him out.'

'It's not so easy. He's very well connected.'

'The bigger they are, the harder they fall — where I come from.'

'What are the options?' said the man in the suit, ignoring the comment, and pushing himself away from the window. 'There's his woman, I suppose. Then there's the girl,' he added. 'Don't forget her.'

'We're on it.'

'Good.'

The man in the suit glanced at his watch and brought the meeting to an end with a curt, 'See to it.'

6

I didn't have to wait long to discover that it wouldn't be at all easy for me to escape the consequences of having visited the South Gare. After I had closed the computer down, I opened the front door and stepped outside for the first time that morning for a breath of fresh air. I saw it immediately. It was impossible to miss.

Someone had draped the body of a large dog — a Labrador, it looked like — across the low wall at the front of my cottage. An iron bar, the kind they use to reinforce concrete, had been driven through its throat to pin it to the wall, and before that, perhaps to kill it. Nasty. There was a lot of blood.

I grimaced and looked round. A big pickup truck straddled the end of the track leading to the road. It looked very like the one I had seen at the South Gare.

The truck's engine started up, as if whoever was in it had been waiting for me to appear. I watched as it roared backwards on to the road in a hail of loose gravel and a cloud of dust. A couple of long blasts on the horn, and then it was away. A point had been made. I had been warned — again!

There was no point trying to follow them, not in my old Land Rover. By the time I got into top gear, they would be out of sight.

So I buried the dog a little distance away and cleaned up. Then I went back inside, wondering what to do for the best. It was disturbing. What the hell had I run into? Clearly, the message left on my phone had not been an idle threat. These people were psychopaths.

I wondered if their appearance so soon after Bill Peart had left was a coincidence or if they had been watching me. Probably the latter. They seemed to be very worried about what I had seen at the South Gare, and what I might do about it.

They had good reason to worry, too, more than ever now. I would have assisted Bill Peart all I could anyway, but this stunt with the dog hadn't done anything to help their cause.

First, though, I needed to talk to Jac about her personal security. She had been named in the phone message. So they were aware of her, and her link to me. I grimaced. This wasn't good for either of us. Much worse for James Campbell, of course.

I couldn't get Jac at home, and if she was at work I didn't want to disrupt her day and upset her with talk of possible threats to her safety. So I left it for the moment. Instead, I phoned the guy from PortPlus who had emailed me. He'd left a direct number, which saved messing about with switchboards and receptionists.

'Mr Rogers?'

'Yeah. How can I help you?'

'Good morning. Frank Doy here. I'm responding to an email you sent me about your company's plans.'

'Ah, yes! Mr Doy. Thank you for calling. I appreciate it.'

An American accent. Expansive style. Early middle-aged, I guessed. Management school type. Corporate man, in other words.

'I was interested in what you said.'

'Good. I'd like to meet you, Mr Doy. As soon as possible. What's your availability like?'

'I'm pretty flexible at the moment. When would suit you?'

I could have said my flexibility was absolute. There was nothing in my diary for a week or two.

'No time like the present. How about today, this afternoon?'

So I wasn't going to be invited to a corporate lunch.

'That's fine,' I told him, hiding my

disappointment. 'See you at two this after-noon.'

*   *   *

So I had lunch with Jac at the usual place, the Italian. She was in a hurry as she was waiting for phone calls from people who had proved hard to get.

'I was just going to have a sandwich,' she said reprovingly once we were sat down.

'You still can.'

'What — here?'

'I don't see why not.'

'Luigi would probably sling us out.'

'Probably.'

I hesitated, being careful, wanting to do this right. I didn't want to upset her but I did want her to understand the situation.

'That business I was telling you about yesterday? The body in the sea?'

'Oh, yes!' She sat up straight. 'Go on. What's happened?'

'They found out who it was. James Campbell, the MP.'

'The local MP?'

I nodded.

'That's terrible!'

All I could do was agree.

'Keep it to yourself for the moment, Jac.

The police haven't announced his death yet.'

'Why not?'

I gave a little grimace. 'It's not as simple as it might have been. He didn't drown, apparently. He was shot first.'

'Murdered?' she asked, wide-eyed.

I nodded. 'Bill Peart's got the case.'

Luigi arrived with the pasta we had ordered. Mine had bacon and onion in it. Hers had bits of sea creatures. I started eating. Jac started picking at hers.

'There's more, isn't there?' she said thoughtfully. 'You haven't told me everything. That's why you wanted to take me out for lunch — when I was so busy, and had already said no twice!'

I chuckled and shook my head. 'Jac Picknett! If you ever get tired of the art business, and are looking for another job, come and see me — please! You'd make a first-class private investigator.'

'If I ever get tired of the art business,' she said, forking a small clam, 'I'm going back to sea, to do some fishing.'

'Rejoin the family line, eh?'

'That's right.'

Jac's family had been fisher folk in Redcar for generations, centuries. Having got out, she was either sensible or a renegade, depending on how you looked at it.

'So?' she said, putting down her fork and staring at me hard.

'So you were right. There's more.' I shrugged. 'When I got home last night there was a message on my phone.'

I told her what had been said, including the fact that her name had been mentioned. I hoped she wasn't too shocked.

'I wanted to warn you,' I concluded, 'not frighten you. Just be aware, Jac. That's all. Bill Peart raised the question of police protection for us. I turned it down. But if you're interested, we can talk to him again about it.'

'No,' she said, as I had expected. 'I don't want that. It's not necessary. Someone threatened you and mentioned my name in passing. So what? Neither of us had anything to do with James Campbell, or with his death. It's tragic, but nothing to do with us. Let's leave it there.'

I nodded. 'My feelings exactly.'

We got on with our meal. It didn't take long. Jac was in a hurry.

I told her about the meeting I was to have that afternoon, to change the subject and lighten the mood as much as anything.

'Any idea what it's about?'

'Not really. But potential new clients are always welcome.'

She looked worried for a moment. 'Take

care, Frank. Don't get involved in anything
. . . shady.'

'Shady?' I laughed. 'Jac, I'm meeting the
CEO of an international company. Besides,
don't I always take care?'

'No,' she said, looking at me with her
serious face on now. 'No, you don't. Most
people go to the South Gare and find the sea
and birds, and things. You go and find a dead
body.'

7

The sense of them being close was unbearable. She couldn't walk any faster. If she did, she would be running!

With a squeal of brakes, a double-decker bus stopped a little way ahead of her. Three people waited to get on board. She began to run to join them.

'Where to?' the driver asked when she got there.

She thrust money at him. 'The terminus.'

She took her change and sat down. No-one had got on after her. For the moment, she felt relieved.

Towns were dangerous, she reflected. As were lots of people. You couldn't see who or what was coming in a town or a crowd.

On the other hand, she had to come out sometimes. She couldn't stay home alone always. He had told her to be careful, which she was being. It was more important than ever to be careful now. She was determined she would be. They were not going to win.

Back there, on the street, they had been close. Somebody had. She had felt it; that prickling in the back of the neck. That sense of being crowded, of someone coming too close. Once, she had almost been sure she had spotted a man, but then he had gone into a shop and she had not seen him again. Still, the feeling had persisted. Perhaps there were others?

She didn't know. What she did know was that she couldn't go home yet. Home was where they had not found her. They didn't even know where she lived. The towns were where she became visible to them. She needed to stay on guard, she told herself, blinking away a tear. The world was a more dangerous place now, and she was alone.

Three stops down the road she got off the bus. The driver seemed surprised but offered no comment. She kept quiet. What could she say? All she knew was that too long on the bus would give them time to recover and find her again. She needed to keep switching tracks frequently. But she couldn't tell the driver that.

This time she hurried through what remained of the old town, heading for the Transporter Bridge. Its gaunt, Meccano-like structure soared high above everything else, but it wasn't height she was seeking. She wanted to cross to the other side, to the sparse openness, and the anonymity, of Port Clarence, where few people who had a choice ventured and where visitors stuck out as if in high-visibility jackets.

8

'We're new to these parts,' Rogers said, 'but we're aiming to make a difference.'

He had already told me what they were about. Surprisingly, to me at least, they were planning a takeover of Teesport, the dock and shipping facilities on the Tees. I nodded and waited patiently for him to make his pitch. The takeover was obviously going to be a big deal, very big. In terms of tonnage handled, Teesport was one of the biggest ports in the country. Fifth in the list, when last I looked, but sometimes second or third. I wondered what the current owners felt about it.

'With our extensive experience of port operations in the United States, as well as elsewhere in the world, we believe we can do great things here. Our stakeholders go along with us on that. Privately perhaps, so do our competitors. We're going to make things really hum!'

He paused to let his secretary deposit a tray of coffee cups on the table. I admired the secretary for a moment. Then I glanced out of the floor-to-ceiling window.

'Great view,' I suggested as he pushed a cup towards me.

'Oh, yes!' he said. 'Yes, indeed.'

He looked out of the window himself and frowned. Good as it was, perhaps it wasn't the same quality of view as he was used to back in the States. If so, I could see where he was coming from.

We were meeting in a new-build office block in the former Ironmasters' District of Middlesbrough, one of the hearths of Victorian industry. Mostly derelict land now, but there were green shoots of recovery poking through the rubble. Riverside House, where PortPlus had its offices, was one of them.

'So,' I said, trying to get my head round what he'd just told me, 'you're looking to buy out the company that owns Teesport, and make a better job of running the port?'

'That's some of it. But we'll do more than that. We plan to make better use of the port's extensive land holdings, too.'

'So where do I come in, Mike?'

We were on first-name terms already. Had been since my arrival. Mike and Frank. Good pals, and potential colleagues, working together. Maybe.

'I'm glad you've brought that up, Frank,' he said earnestly. 'The way I see it, you're just the guy we need.'

He paused, sipped his coffee and eyed me thoughtfully.

'As I'm sure you can imagine, there's a lot we need to do in advance of the acquisition. No sensible business goes into a new venture without a whole lot of research preceding the purchase. Due diligence, right?'

'Right.' I shrugged. 'Not really my field, Mike.'

He nodded and moved on. 'One of the things we need is a strategic overview of the port operation in terms of security and safety requirements. In short, we want to know what the risks are, where the weaknesses are, what the threats might be — and, most importantly, what can be done to anticipate and defend against them. That's where you come in, Frank.'

'A big job,' I suggested, slightly unnerved by the scale of what he was unfolding.

'Indeed it is. But we think you're the man for it.'

I wasn't so sure about that, but I wasn't going to say so right at the outset. I wanted to hear the man out, and give myself some thinking time.

'You don't have your own people to do this sort of work?'

'We do have security staff, of course. You can't run ports without them, given all the opportunities for theft, smuggling, illegal import-export, and the like — never mind terrorism. But in this situation we lack local knowledge, and local knowledge is key. That's what we want you to provide.'

'In relation to . . . what, exactly?'

'Fencing, security patrols, electronic barriers, people investigation systems — whatever seems important at a strategic level. We're not going to tell you what to look for, Frank, or what to do. What we will do, however, is pay top dollar for your expertise and local knowledge.'

I nodded, impressed. I would need to scope the job properly before I took it on, but there could be a lot in this for me. It was a big, and potentially lucrative, contract he was waving at me.

'You want to talk figures?' he asked. 'Money?'

I shook my head. 'Not yet, Mike. I need to think about what you've said and work out how best to approach the job. We can talk about the price later.'

'Fine,' he said with a nod.

'Well, I've got enough information for now, I think.'

'Good. Get back to me as soon as you can, Frank. We're in a hurry.'

Just then the door opened and an older man looked into the room. Rogers looked round, surprised, and then he smiled.

'Ah, Donovan!' he said, recovering fast.

'Just the guy I wanted to see. Come in and meet Frank Doy. I'm hoping he'll be doing our strategic overview of security issues. Frank, meet Donovan McCardle, our chairman.'

I stood up to shake hands with the newcomer.

'Mr Doy. I'm pleased to meet you,' he said in a rich, deep voice. 'Are you going to take the job?'

He didn't sound American, as I would have expected. If anything, his accent behind the smooth tone sounded antipodean. Certainly not local anyway.

'I'm going to go away and work out what I can do for you, Mr McCardle. It's a very interesting opportunity Mike has just outlined, and I hope I can rise to the challenge.'

'Good. Excellent.'

He nodded and smiled in a perfunctory way, giving me the impression his heart wasn't in it. But he was a very courteous, civilized sort of man, one who perhaps came from old money rather than one who had made his way up through management schools and the lower echelons of the corporate world. Quiet authority had entered the room with him.

'When you're finished with Mr Doy, Mike, I'd like a word,' he said, moving on.

'I'm just on my way out,' I volunteered,

turning towards the door.

'I'll hear from you . . . ?' Rogers asked.

'Soon,' I said. 'In a couple of days.'

We all shook hands. Then I left, wondering if I had ever come across Donovan McCardle before. Something about him had seemed vaguely familiar. I would never have forgotten a name or a face like his, but I just couldn't place him at all.

9

She paid for her ticket and joined the four cars and half-dozen pedestrians and cyclists also making the trip. Together with the others, she stood on the cradle — the gondola, they called it — that hung suspended from the roof of the structure and waited for it to complete its gentle progress across the Tees.

On the other side, the cars and her fellow passengers all sped off immediately. She waited. She stood out of the way, beside an old brick wall, and waited. She waited five minutes, ten. Two cars and a small lorry boarded the gondola for the return journey. She hadn't seen any of them before. She hadn't seen the two cyclists who joined them before either. When the bridge captain came to close the gates in readiness for departure, she jogged forward and slipped aboard.

The gondola set off back across the river. She stayed out of sight but kept her eyes focussed on the opposite bank. Complacency had never been one of her failings. Neither had impatience. You couldn't be a hunter without patience and mental stamina, and you couldn't survive being hunted, a hunt victim, without them either.

Her eyesight was good, excellent in fact. She saw the man when they were only halfway across the river. She had never knowingly seen him before but she knew he was waiting for her.

So she couldn't go home yet.

★   ★   ★

A woman sat behind the wheel of one of the cars. She approached her and asked if she would mind giving her a lift to the railway station, claiming to be afraid of missing her train. The woman smiled and opened the door for her.

As they left the gondola, she kept her head down, and believed the man missed her.

At the railway station she thanked the woman and went inside, only to come back out again almost immediately. A bus stopped nearby. She saw the destination was Stockton, a couple of miles to the west. She boarded the bus. Going in the opposite direction seemed a sensibly counter-intuitive thing to do. The fox does that, she thought with a wry smile, when he runs down the centre of the road instead of crossing it. Confusing the hunt. That was the idea.

★ ★ ★

She didn't know how it happened, but in Stockton she found herself near the river again. There, she mingled with students roaming through a complex of buildings that turned out to be the university campus. Still wandering, she came across a rowing club. There were one or two boats, sculls she supposed they would be called, on the river. Even more were alongside the river, pulled out of the water, sitting in neat rows, ready for use. And then she came across a group of kayaks, also in waiting.

Her mind raced. How far? No distance at all. Ten or twelve miles, perhaps. No more. She thought about the current and the tide. She would be going with the flow. No incoming tide to work against. Even after the barrage she could see a little distance away the tide would be in her favour. The river would carry her there. All she had to do was steer.

Her excitement grew. This was how she could elude them. They would never think of it. She hadn't even thought of it herself until now. A last quick look round. Then she stepped off the path and stooped to push one of the kayaks into the water.

10

By the time I got out of the building, the first doubts were surfacing. What Mike Rogers had been talking about was a big job. Could I handle it? Possibly, but doing it properly would take time. Months, probably. PortPlus wouldn't want that; they had come to me because they thought my local knowledge would allow me to do the job fast.

But perhaps I had that wrong? Perhaps they knew it could only be a superficial job if it was done fast, and that was all they wanted anyway? It certainly made more sense to look at it that way.

It was still puzzling that they had come to me in the first place. Who had given them my name? And why had they decided I was the man for the job? I owed somebody a pint, and perhaps more.

I shook my head and dived into the Duke of Wellington. I ordered a guest ale I'd never heard of to allay my unease about the job.

Quite apart from the scale and speed of what was required, I hadn't much liked the PortPlus CEO. He was too much Corporate Man for my taste. Mr Smooth-and-Clean.

Suit and tie, and parachuted in from a million miles away. A bean counter at heart. Not my kind of person.

But the job would keep the wolf from the door for many months, I reminded myself. So maybe I should just swallow my reservations, and get on with it. Plenty of my clients were people I didn't much care for in a personal sense.

Having begun to rationalize the situation to my own satisfaction, I called Jac to let her know how the meeting had gone.

'Frank? Thank God! I've been trying to phone you all afternoon,' she said without preamble. 'There was no answer.'

'I switched my phone off before I went into the meeting. Why? What's the matter?'

'I'm worried, Frank. A neighbour phoned to say some strange men were around my house. When I dashed home to see what was going on, they were very unpleasant. Quite frightening, really. And they made threats concerning you.'

My pulse was racing long before she had finished.

'Are you all right, Jac?'

'I suppose so. More or less.'

'Have they gone?'

'I think so.'

'Stay where you are. If you see them again, phone the police. I'll get there as fast as I can

48

— twenty minutes, or so.'

I got up, abandoning my pint. An elderly drinker at a nearby table looked round as he heard my chair scrape and said, 'I didn't think much of that beer either, son. Go and complain. They'll give you another one.'

I nodded and made for the door. The last thing I needed was well-meant advice about beer.

★   ★   ★

'So what happened?'

Jac looked at me and shrugged. 'Nothing,' she said. 'They didn't trash the house or beat me up. They were rough men, and they just . . . just terrified me!'

We sat in the kitchen and I made a pot of tea. Jac was composed now but unusually withdrawn.

'What did they say?'

'They said I should remind you to say nothing about what you saw the other day at the South Gare. If I did that, and you did that, nothing would happen to either of us.'

'That it?'

She nodded. 'It was the way they looked at me that was so frightening. The one that spoke just radiated power and evil.'

I was in no doubt how upset she was. I had

never seen her like this. It had been a bad experience, one I had brought on her, however inadvertently.

'Three of them, you said?'

She nodded.

They must have been the three I had seen at the Gare. Witness intimidation was obviously their priority right now, and they were doing pretty well. I didn't tell Jac what they had done to the dog. That wouldn't have helped.

'They've gone now,' I said gently. 'They won't be back. But come and stay with me for a while?'

She shook her head, paused a moment and then said, 'I can't do this, Frank. I can't live like this. It's all right for you. You're used to it. But I'm not — and I don't want to be!'

I could sense she wasn't going to stop now. I waited, tense, wondering what else was going to come out.

'I've been thinking,' she said, taking a deep breath and slowing down, 'and I've come to the conclusion that I don't want to continue with our relationship. I'm sorry, Frank, but I like the life I've built for myself, and it's under threat now because of my relationship with you.'

She hadn't finished yet either. She shrugged and added, 'It's just one thing after another. I want to spend my time thinking about painters and paintings, not worrying about criminals and threats to my life!'

I knew then that nothing I could say would make any difference. Anyway, she was right. I knew that, as well.

'So what do you want to do?' I asked wearily.

'I want all this to end. I've decided to go away for a while. You can get on with your life, and I'll get on with mine. Oh, I know it's not your fault, Frank! You didn't go to the South Gare the other day and decide to get involved in whatever was going on there. It just happened. I do know that. I don't blame you. But these things happen too often around you — you seem to attract them! And I can't live in a permanent danger zone.'

So there we were. This wasn't what I wanted. But it was what she wanted, and I knew it was probably right for her. Once I had come to terms with that, there wasn't a lot more to be said.

'When are you leaving?'

She glanced up at the clock on the kitchen wall and said, 'As soon as the taxi arrives.'

I didn't bother asking her where she was going, or for how long. I didn't give her any advice either. I just kissed her on the cheek and walked out.

★ ★ ★

I headed home after that. I was feeling low, really low, as down as I had been for a long time. Jac was right. I knew that. This was no way to live. Bill Peart had told me the same thing often enough. So had Jimmy Mack, my neighbour and friend, if it came to that. Trouble was never far away from me. Why would any sane, decent person want to be anywhere near?

But this was what I did. It was how I made my living and stayed free, my own man. There were bad times but there were also the good times, and I got a buzz out of them. Low as I was at that moment, I knew I wasn't going to change.

★ ★ ★

They were waiting for me when I got back to Risky Point. The pickup that was becoming increasingly familiar was parked at my gate.

I stopped, hesitated a moment and then got out. So did they. I recognized them. They were the three from the South Gare.

'What do you want?' I demanded.

'Nothing, bonnie lad,' the leader replied with a confident smile. 'We just came by to see how you were getting on. Keeping in touch, you know.'

Not local. He was a Geordie, by the sound of it.

'You're a long way from home,' I pointed out.

'We like to see how you folk in the country live.'

'I hear you were in Redcar a little earlier, as well?'

'Were we?'

'Threatening a friend of mine.'

He chuckled. 'Oh, yes! Your lady friend. Nice, isn't she? Nice house, as well. Be a pity if anything happens to her.'

'Get out of here!'

I was angry by then, seething in fact, but not yet mad enough to ignore the way the odds were stacked against me. I headed straight for my front door.

'Hang on, Doy! We want to talk.'

'One moment,' I told him over my shoulder. 'Don't go away.'

I went inside. When I came back out I was carrying a loaded shotgun.

'Now, what do you want to talk about?'

'No need for that,' the leader said easily, not intimidated. 'Why would you fetch a thing like that?'

'Say what you've got to say, and then get out.'

He looked me in the eye and nodded. 'Be

careful, Doy. That's the message. Don't do anything, or say anything, that could come back to cause you or your lady friend trouble.'

'What did you have against Campbell?' I asked. 'That's what's been puzzling me.'

'Forget him. Forget you were ever there — you've been told!'

'Another question,' I said. 'Who are you working for?'

That seemed to amuse them for some reason. All three smiled at that. The big guy looked at the others before turning back to me and shaking his head.

'What are you like?' he said wonderingly. 'Questions, questions, questions!'

'I've got plenty more, as well!'

'Well, it's been nice meeting you, Doy. We've enjoyed seeing where you live, out here in the beautiful countryside.'

His tone changed as he added, 'Just don't make us come back again. Keep your mouth shut — and stay away from the cops!'

He turned, and led the way back to their vehicle. It was a bit cleaner than it had been the first time I'd seen it. I could see the markings on the side now. It belonged to a hire company.

11

The man in the suit said to his boss, 'It's worrying.'

'You worry too much!'

'Maybe so, but I think we should call those other guys back.'

'I thought you had men on it?'

'I do, but . . . '

'They're not good enough?'

The man in the suit shrugged. 'Who knows? Maybe not. There's the girl, as well, remember?'

His boss grimaced and admitted, 'I worry about her, too. She's a real loose cannon.'

'I don't know about that, but suddenly we seem to have a lot of loose ends.'

The boss hesitated, thought about it and then said, 'You're right. We'll call them back if we have to, but let's just carry on as we are for a bit longer.'

'We haven't got a lot of time, remember?'

'Give it a bit longer. Pressure can work wonders, if you give it a chance.'

12

I tried to put all the nonsense aside and con-
centrate on work. Jac had taken herself out of
the picture. So I didn't need to worry about
her. And I certainly wasn't going to spend
time worrying about three ugly Geordies who
were dangerous enough but not very smart. I
phoned Bill Peart to tell him about my encounter with them. I also gave him the name of the
hire company that owned the truck.

'A Tyneside company, eh?'

'Presumably. It was a 0191 number, anyway.'

'We'll get on it. You OK?'

'I'm fine.'

'And Jac?'

'She's taking a holiday, Bill. She's well out
of it. There's no need for her to put up with
crap like this.'

'Quite right, too. We'll find them,' he
assured me.

'I hope you do. You'll not solve James
Campbell's murder without them.'

'Meanwhile,' Bill said, 'we'll keep an eye on
Jac's house.'

★ ★ ★

Back to work. PortPlus. I needed to know more about them. Correction: I needed to know something about them. All I knew so far was what I had heard from Mike Rogers, and that wasn't enough. Apart from anything else, before I did any work for them I needed to know if they could pay me. It's always worth checking. I've found that the hard way.

Googling didn't produce much. But names sometimes don't mean much these days. They can be instant creations without any substance behind them. Just names. What you need to know is what organization spawned them, or whose is the money behind them.

The PortPlus people, for all I knew, could have a five per cent holding in one port, twenty per cent in another, and thirty per cent in something else. They didn't have to own anything outright. Also, theirs didn't have to be the name up there in lights.

Still . . . After half an hour I began to wonder what PortPlus was. I couldn't find anything about them. It was beginning to be worrying.

★　★　★

A thunderous knocking on the door told me my neighbour, Jimmy Mack, had come to distract me. I gave up on the computer search and switched on the kettle instead.

'What have you been up to?' he asked suspiciously when I opened the door.

'Me? Nothing. Why?'

I let him inside and he seized the best of the kitchen chairs, the only one that doesn't creak and threaten to fall apart when you sit on it.

'Coffee, Jim?'

He nodded. 'You haven't been around much lately?'

'No. I've been busy.'

'You won't have heard the news, then?'

'What news?'

'One of them politicians fell off the breakwater at the South Gare and drowned himself. Supposedly.'

Jimmy gave me a speculative look.

'I did know that, actually,' I admitted. 'So they've released the story, have they?'

He nodded, and looked satisfied to have wrung the admission out of me.

'Your mate Bill Peart was on the television, talking about it. He didn't say an awful lot, mind, as usual.'

Bill was a pretty frequent visitor to Risky Point and my cranky old fisherman neighbour knew him well enough.

'So what's your problem with that?' I asked as I made the coffee.

Jimmy chuckled sarcastically and shook his head. 'It doesn't make sense, does it? A man like that, a politician, going to the end of the breakwater at the height of a spring tide?'

'Maybe he wanted to see the full glory of the sea in all its majesty — or something?'

'With no cameras there? A politician?'

He was quite astute, old Jimmy, as well as cynical.

'Anyway,' he added, 'I'd have thought he was too busy. He's the one that's been making so much fuss about everything — geese, seals, wind turbines, the Redcar steelworks, unemployment . . . There's no end to his protests and campaigns — all for good causes, though. I'll give him that.'

I had to smile. Jim had summed him up pretty well.

'So what do you think happened to him?'

He looked at me sternly and shook his head. 'All I know is he didn't fall off the breakwater, not all by himself he didn't.'

I realized then that I had to tell him something. Living next to me, and with no other neighbours for a couple of miles, he would be vulnerable if the Geordies, and the mystery caller behind them, decided to make good on their threats and promises.

'You're not wrong, Jim.'

'Ah!'

Again, he looked satisfied with himself.

'He was shot first, apparently. Bill Peart told me — in confidence. They didn't want that information to go public just yet, though.'

Jimmy nodded. 'When I saw Bill on the telly, I wondered where you came in. You had to be involved somehow.'

'Unfortunately, I found the body. At least, I was the one who saw the body in the water and alerted the police.' I hesitated and then added, 'There were three blokes nearby who I suspected had put him there. I'm telling you this, Jim, because a threatening message was left on my phone, warning me to keep out of it. I've also had callers at my door bringing the same message. So has Jac.

'So keep your eyes open. Watch out for yourself — but don't get involved! I've told Jac that, as well. I don't want either of you in harm's way.'

He slurped his coffee and then wiped his mouth with the back of his hand.

'What's wrong?' I asked, seeing the look of anguish on his face.

'Is there any sugar at all in this?'

I dived into a cupboard and pulled out a few sachets I'd picked up somewhere and kept for the likes of Jimmy.

'Anything else?' I demanded.

Patiently, he tore open one sachet after another, emptying the contents into his mug.

'Just one thing,' he said steadily. 'What were you doing there, at the South Gare, when he fell in the water?'

'I've asked myself that same question.'

'I mean, it's not as if you're short of trouble, is it?'

I shook my head. He wasn't wrong about that.

13

She brought the kayak ashore at last. It had been a longer and more tiring journey than she had expected, and she was stiff and drained from the unaccustomed exercise. The mental strain had been considerable, too, especially as darkness had descended.

First, she'd had to find a way round the Tees Barrage, which had meant leaving the water and hauling and carrying the kayak until she was clear. Then, in the lower reaches of the river, there had been big ships to avoid, as well as launches and cutters, fishing boats and oil industry vessels. None of them could have noticed her. She'd had to be watchful, and sometimes take evasive action, to keep herself out of harm's way. No, not an easy journey at all.

Somehow she'd made it, and here she was at the mouth of the river. She climbed gingerly out of the kayak and into water that reached over her knees. Then she stood still and glanced round cautiously, but it was dark and there was nobody to see her. She stooped, took hold of the fragile craft and hauled it up onto a bank of shingle. Then she spent a few minutes stretching to work the stiffness out of her limbs.

Nearly home! she thought with satisfaction as she straightened up. And there was no way they could have followed her. She was safe at last.

She studied the kayak, wondering what to do about it. Her first inclination was to sink it and get rid of it. But it wasn't hers, and anyway who could tell when it might come in useful again? So she dragged it up the bank and into a clump of elder bushes. That done, she set off to run the last little way through the dunes, exhausted but relieved and happy to be safely back home.

Later, recovering, she reflected on how difficult it was now she was alone. He had warned her it would be, but back then she hadn't taken much notice. She had been so happy with what he was giving her. Besides, she couldn't believe that either of them could possibly come to harm. Now she needed to come to terms with how wrong she had been.

It wasn't over yet either, she thought moodily. Far from it. It was getting worse by the day. They were hunting her. She knew that for sure now. They couldn't just let her be. She wished bitterly that she had never gone to confront them, although that might not have saved her. She knew too much.

And she was alone now, she reminded herself again. There was just her. Maybe she wouldn't be able to manage — it would prove too much for her? It was quite possible.

Oh, if only she had a partner! She really needed someone to shoulder some of the burden.

Fat chance of that, of course. She would just have to do it alone. And she would, too. There was no choice. She wanted to make him proud of her, wherever he was now.

She sniffed away a tear and blew out the candle. Then, wearily, she lay down. She had done enough for one day.

14

Although I needed to get to grips with scoping the job for PortPlus, Jimmy Mack's visit had unsettled me. Once again, I was wondering what I had stumbled into at the South Gare. Who was behind the three men who had terrified Jac, and come to lean on me? Who was pulling the strings? And why had a serving Member of Parliament been murdered anyway?

I knew what Bill Peart would have said: Keep out of it! Leave it to us. That's what we're paid to do, answer questions like that.

As Jimmy had pointed out, though, I was involved, and had been almost from the start. So I couldn't leave it alone. The threats made to me and to Jac had had the effect of interesting me more than ever, not putting me off. Without them, I might just have got on with my own business, and left Bill Peart to deal with his. As it was, I couldn't let go.

It had all started with James Campbell. Someone had taken exception to him, or to what he was doing. Of all the things he had been involved with, what was it that had made him so insufferable that he had to be eliminated?

★ ★ ★

The next morning I decided to contact the constituency office of the Labour Party, thinking Campbell's agent might have an idea of what it was all about. I had got his name from a piece in the local paper about the recent elections.

The woman that answered the phone said they were too busy to talk. In any case, she added, there was no-one there on such a sad day. It seemed a bit of a contradiction, but I let it go. Probably they were all stunned and uncertain what to do with themselves.

I visited them anyway. When I got there, nobody was busy. There were just three or four people sitting around drinking coffee and looking miserable.

'Jack Gregory?' I asked.

A middle-aged woman in jeans and a washed-out Michael Jackson T-shirt looked up and said, 'Sorry. He's not available. What do you want?'

It was a bad time to be calling, but it was a bad time for me as well as for them. So I just said, 'I want to talk about James Campbell.'

'We're all too busy,' the woman said,

shaking her head. 'I'm sorry, but we can't be dealing with you today.'

A middle-aged man in a well-worn, charcoal-grey suit looked at me dolefully but didn't say anything.

'Shut the door on your way out,' a feisty young woman wearing a duffle coat said.

Finally, the other member of the group came to life. A young guy in jeans and sweater, he stood up and said, 'I'm Jack Gregory. Come on through.'

He turned and led the way out of the front office to his retreat at the end of a corridor.

'Don't mind that lot,' he said wearily over his shoulder. 'We're all pretty down today.'

'I understand.'

He was maybe thirty, or so, and seemed full of energy even on a day like that. I judged he was glad to have a break from the wake they were holding in the front office.

'Frank Doy,' I told him once we were sat down. 'I won't piss you about, Jack. I'm aware of what's happened, and I can see how upset everyone is. I'm a private investigator and security consultant. But I don't mean to be insensitive, and I'll not take up much of your time.'

'Time is what we have at the moment,' he said with a sigh. 'Our world has come to a stop. What do you want to know?'

'I would like to find out what local issues James was working on. A potential inward investor has asked me to produce an overview of what's happening in the area, and this seemed a good place to start. I hoped you might be able to brief me on how James saw the problems and opportunities in his constituency.'

Gregory developed a frown and a slight flush. Anger seemed to be bubbling to the surface.

'At a time like this?' he said. 'And you don't want to be insensitive?'

I decided to take a gamble. It was either that or get thrown out.

'Ask me why it matters — to me, personally,' I said.

He stared hard for a moment and then said, 'Go on — why?'

'I was the one who found his body.'

That shut him up.

'At least,' I added, 'I was the one who saw him in the sea and called the police.'

He sucked in his breath. 'What were you doing there?'

'Nothing.' I shook my head. 'It was pure coincidence. I just happened to be visiting the South Gare that afternoon. When I got there, it can't have been long after he'd gone into the sea.'

'And you had nothing to do with it, I take it?'

'Nothing at all.'

'Expect me to believe that?'

He was on guard and feisty. Sick to the stomach and mad as hell, probably. And now I'd arrived with what probably sounded like a fantasy tale.

'Tell you what, Jack. I'm a personal friend of DI Bill Peart who is investigating this case. I'll give you his direct line. You can ring him and get him to confirm what I've just told you. That good enough?'

It took a few moments. Then he nodded and said, 'OK. I know Peart. He's a good man. I'll take your word for it. Do you want a coffee, by the way?'

'That would be good.'

'On second thoughts,' he added, glancing at the clock on the wall, 'let's go and have a drink. I'm bloody sick of this place already today.'

★　★　★

We went to the White Swan just round the corner. It wasn't a pub I frequented, although it had always been there.

'Very retro,' I suggested, looking round at the plastic-covered bench seats and the formica tables, along with walls thick with layers of cream emulsion on top of woodchip wallpaper.

'Yeah.' He looked round himself and nodded with satisfaction. 'Circa 1959, would you say?'

'Even earlier. Mid-fifties, I would guess.'

'Probably.' He nodded again and added, 'They keep a good beer, though. What are you having?'

'Let me get them. I've interrupted your morning.'

'Thanks. I'll have the Steel Special.'

'Appropriate choice for here, especially today.'

He nodded and slumped onto a seat.

'So you want to know what James was working on?' he asked when I returned from the bar. 'You being a private investigator?'

'Well . . . On a personal level, I'm involved, like it or not. I want to know what happened — why and how he died. Then, as I explained, I've been asked by a big potential investor to brief them on what's happening around here. Difficult strategic issues, and so on. The two things come together for me: Campbell was an important man in these parts, and from what I can make out, he was aware of everything that's going on.'

He nodded and took a swig of his beer. I

followed suit. He was right. The beer was good here.

'What James was working on?' Jack murmured thoughtfully. 'You're right — everything! I couldn't keep up with him. He was working on every bloody thing in the world!'

'I gathered that,' I admitted with a smile.

'I wanted him to pull back a bit and focus more, but he couldn't do that. He couldn't let anything go. If someone raised an issue, or if he could see something that needed doing, he just went for it flat out.'

'He must have been a busy guy.'

Jack grinned. 'Hell on wheels!'

'Was there anything in particular lately? Anything really important, or particularly controversial?'

'One or two things, actually.' Jack frowned and studied his beer for a moment. 'He was a good man, you know. We all loved him. I can't believe he's gone. It's been a hell of a shock.'

I nodded. I wasn't surprised. It was too soon, really, to be asking him questions, but I had a sense that things were moving, and moving fast, and I wanted to get on with it.

'Environmental issues were big with him,' Jack said thoughtfully. 'There were rumours and he was worried to death the port authority was going to do something crass — like try to develop on the Seal Sands

71

nature reserve, or want to build a nuclear power station on the south side of the river to match the one at Hartlepool on the other side.'

That caught my attention. Rumours? I wondered if they were anything to do with PortPlus and their plans.

'Was that why he was at the South Gare on that particular day?' I asked. 'Was he supposed to be meeting someone there?'

Jack shrugged. 'No idea. He hadn't told me he was going there. And it wasn't in his diary. As a matter of fact, he didn't have any commitments that day. He'd deliberately kept it clear. I don't know what he had in mind.'

'It's an interesting old place, the South Gare,' I mused, thinking about it. 'Run-down and dilapidated, and minus a lot of the functions it used to have, but still with a role to play.'

'Yeah?'

'It was built to channel the river through the estuary, and it still does that. Then there's the fishermen's huts, the yacht club in the old army base — not to mention the lighthouse, and what not.'

He nodded, but I could tell he'd lost interest. He swallowed a lot of his pint in one go, looked at me and said, 'Know what I think?'

I shook my head.

'They seem to think it was an accident or suicide, but it wasn't.'

'No?'

'I'm sure they'll find it was murder.'

He wasn't wrong, but I couldn't tell him so. Not yet. If Bill Peart hadn't already told him, it wasn't for me to do so.

'That's a big leap, Jack.'

'Not really. He'd had death threats. Plenty of them. Some, especially lately, were quite worrying.'

'What about?'

'You name it!' He shrugged. 'Cranks, self-interest groups, money men, campaign groups.'

'Nothing in particular?'

'Mostly, I suppose, they had to do with things along the river. Environmentalists fearful about more development, and business and jobs people frustrated by environmental concerns.'

'Standard stuff, then?'

'Yeah. Mostly.' He frowned. 'But not all of it. Some of it was just plain nasty and personal.'

He suddenly thought of something, looked at me and said, 'Who did you say you were working for?'

'I didn't. I'm not working for anyone yet, but a company has asked me to do some work for them and I'm thinking about it.'

'Who are they?'

I hesitated. Client confidentiality, and all that. But what the hell! I was just considering the job. I hadn't actually taken it yet.

'An outfit called PortPlus. They're American, I think.'

Jack Gregory scowled. 'Bunch of shitheads! Don't touch 'em with a bargepole. They were one of James' biggest problems.'

'Why?'

'I'm not sure.' He frowned. 'Until very recently, James was all for them, and what they wanted to do. Then he turned against them, and was about to start campaigning to try to stop them. All I knew was that the whole business had taken his eye off the ball. All sorts of things were being neglected because of his preoccupation with PortPlus.'

He glanced at the big clock on the wall, sighed and grimaced. 'I'm sorry. I'd better get back to the office. They'll be thinking I've abandoned ship.'

★ ★ ★

I walked Jack back to his office, and shook his hand and thanked him for his time.

'Let me know how you get on,' he said. 'I'm interested. Meantime, nice meeting you.

Excuse me,' he added, half-turning towards the girl I'd seen in the office wearing a duffel coat, who was now coming down the front steps. 'I need to have a word with Nancy before she leaves.'

I turned away and set off back to my car, running what he had told me through my head, trying to sort the wheat from the chaff. I hadn't gone more than twenty yards when I was interrupted.

'Hey!'

I turned round. The girl in the duffel coat had almost caught up with me.

I nodded. 'Hello?'

'What do you want to know about James Campbell?' she asked bluntly.

'What makes you think . . . ?'

'I heard you in the office. I'm Nancy Peters,' she said, holding out her hand. 'Buy me a coffee and I'll tell you everything I know.'

15

We found a craft shop that also served coffee. Judging by the way she led me there and spoke to the woman behind the counter, Nancy knew it well. It suited her, too. With her coat, she looked as if she belonged somewhere like that, a craft shop — or a charity shop. But she was a good-looking woman, all the same.

'Nice coat,' I said, eyeing her voluminous duffel as we sat down. It looked a bit shabby, and several sizes too big for her. But what do I know?

'It's original, too,' she said, brushing a hand down the front and giving me a smile.

'From when you were in the navy?'

'Something like that.'

She slipped the coat off her shoulders. Beneath it she was wearing an old T-shirt and jeans. The T-shirt slogan indicated she was intent on saving the planet.

'So you knew James Campbell?' I said, once we had taken delivery of our coffees.

'Very well.' She had asked for black coffee, and now she stirred it vigorously. 'What do you want to know?'

'Do you work in the constituency office?' I countered.

She shook her head. 'I know them all there, though.'

'Including Jack Gregory?'

'Of course.'

She stopped stirring at last, raised the mug and sipped her coffee. 'I heard you say you wanted to talk about James?' she said, squinting at me, suddenly looking close to tears.

'That's right. I did.'

I left it there for the moment. I was still wondering who she was, and why she had come after me. She could have spoken to me inside the office.

'James Campbell's death must have been a terrible shock to you all?' I suggested.

'It certainly was.' She grimaced and looked down. 'The worst possible thing to happen. A good many people will suffer because of it.'

'So what's your own interest?' I asked.

'What's yours?' she responded quickly, aggressively.

I hesitated but I knew I would have to give her something if we were to keep talking. By then, I was sufficiently intrigued with her to want to know what she knew.

'I saw his body in the sea,' I said gently. 'I was the one who called the police. Since then,

I've been threatened and warned to keep quiet. So I'm involved. But I'm not easily frightened off, and I want to know what's been going on.'

She stared hard at me, her mouth open with astonishment.

'Did you see what happened?' she demanded after a moment.

I shook my head.

Still she stared.

'It wasn't me who put him there either,' I said. 'Just in case you're wondering.'

She grimaced. 'Poor James! You told Jack all this?'

'I did, yes.'

She sat back and closed her eyes for a moment. Then she rocked forward and fixed me with a keen look.

'It wasn't an accident,' she said firmly, wiping her eyes with the back of her hand. 'It wasn't suicide either.'

'What makes you say that?'

'I have my reasons.'

'Well, you're right on both counts,' I told her, abandoning all caution. 'He was murdered. He didn't drown.'

That made her stare at me harder than ever.

'So how did he die?' she asked through compressed lips.

'He was shot. Then his body was dumped in the sea.'

'You sure?'

I nodded and said I was.

It probably wasn't wise to be telling her all this but the news would be out soon enough anyway, if it hadn't already happened. The police couldn't keep the lid on it forever. Besides, I needed to make progress, and for that to happen I had to offer incentives and give more out. So far, I'd got nowhere, and it was bugging the hell out of me.

'Who are you?' she asked suddenly.

'Frank Doy. I'm a private investigator and security consultant, amongst other things. I had no prior connection to James Campbell. I just happened to be in the wrong place at the time.'

'You seem to know a lot of stuff. Do you have contact with the police?'

I nodded.

We sat in silence for a few moments. I sensed she was processing what I had just told her, as well as trying to decide what to make of me. I was doing the same thing about her.

'A private investigator?' she said, looking up almost hopefully. 'You may be just what I need.'

'Oh?'

'All this is just what I expected to happen. I told him — I warned him! But he wouldn't be told. Oh, no! Not James, not him. He was more concerned about me than himself.'

She lapsed back into a brooding silence. Just as I was wondering how to get her out of it, she came back to life and looked at me.

'He was a good man,' she said sadly, 'a very good man. Too good for here, and the likes of us.'

She looked away again, and I was moved. That statement had come from the heart. For the first time, I felt empathy towards the man. He was becoming a human being to me, not just a victim, and I seemed to have met someone who had cared a lot about him.

'Tell me more about him,' I said gently. 'What was he like?'

'He was a lovely man. Everyone who knew him agreed about that.' She shrugged. 'What more can I say? He spent his life helping people. Nothing was too much trouble for him.'

'Did he help you?'

'He was trying to.'

'That how you knew him?'

'Well . . . Sort of.'

She was upset and seemed close to tears. I didn't press her.

The woman from behind the counter came with the coffee jug and offered us refills. I hesitated, but Nancy said yes. So I went along with her.

'Why was James concerned about you?' I asked.

She just shrugged.

'You said he was, remember?'

Now she shrugged impatiently. 'He was concerned about me because I was around him so much. He didn't want any trouble to rub off onto me.'

'And could it have done? Did it, in fact?'

She shrugged again. 'Possibly. But it's nothing I can't handle,' she added defiantly.

'You sound just like James must have done when you spoke to him!'

Now she gave a rueful smile, but she didn't add anything.

'If you are in any sort of danger, don't hesitate to go to the police.'

'Sure. Good advice.'

'I mean it.'

'Yeah.'

She was recovering, and I was beginning to think I'd got everything I was going to get out of Nancy Peters. James Campbell had been a nice man, and she was very upset about his death. It was time I left her to it and went searching elsewhere.

'I keep a boat at the South Gare,' she said suddenly.

81

'A sail boat?'

'A coble. I fish.'

'Really?' I was surprised. 'For fun?'

'For a living,' she said with a shrug. Then she smiled and added ruefully, 'It's not a very good living.'

Now I was astonished.

There was a fisherman's community at the South Gare, with about fifty wooden huts tucked away in the sand dunes and a number of boats moored in nearby Paddy's Hole, a little haven carved out of the slag on the river side of the breakwater.

'Where do you keep the boat? Paddy's Hole?'

'Yes. It was my grandfather's. My dad's father's. I inherited it — along with this coat!' she added with a smile. 'I have a hut down there, as well.'

'Was this anything to do with your knowing James?'

'Sort of . . . I suppose,' she admitted, petering out.

After a moment I added, 'I think I read somewhere that the huts are under threat?'

'Well, the whole of the South Gare is. That's partly why James was concerned.'

'Where's the threat coming from?'

'An overseas investor is supposed to be interested in taking over the port — and the river and everything associated with it. Haven't you heard?'

'Something. I've heard bits and pieces. Do you know who it is?'

'Some cowboy outfit called PortPlus, or something equally stupid.'

So there it was, out in the open. This was the second person I had spoken to who had named names. I knew now I had a problem. Another one.

'Who did you say you were working for?' she asked.

'I didn't.'

When she sat waiting patiently, her big liquid eyes fixed on me, I added, 'PortPlus, of course.'

'Of course,' she said, suddenly looking thoroughly disillusioned with me, the world and everything in it.

16

I didn't get any further with Nancy Peters.
She didn't know what to make of me after
hearing of my link with PortPlus, and I
doubted if she knew anything significant
anyway. After I left her, I went home feeling
pretty dispirited.

As soon as I reached the cottage, I saw the
signs and I didn't like them. Just little things.
But I saw them, and recognized them for
what they were. Somebody had been here.
Somebody had been inside my house.

The first thing I noticed was the faint
impression of a shoe sole on the top step
leading up to the front door. It wasn't mine,
and it wasn't Jimmy Mack's either. And
no-one would stand on that top step unless
they were going into the house. Not even the
postman, or someone distributing circulars.
The letter box was at the gate.

I frowned and made my way inside, senses
alert. After shutting the door, I stood still and
listened for a few moments. Nothing. Just the
heavy ticking of the wall clock in the kitchen
and the hum of the fridge. Nothing out of the
ordinary.

I moved on systematically, taking one room at a time. There was no-one here now. But there had been. I could smell him on the air. And I could see where he had been.

It wasn't much, but it was enough. The door to the spare bedroom was closed; I always left it open to allow the air to circulate and ward off damp. The computer felt ever so slightly warm, even though I hadn't used it since early that morning. The sliding door on the wardrobe in my bedroom was open six inches. I kept it at two, just enough to allow some air to circulate. You notice these things when you live alone.

Someone had been through my house.

★   ★   ★

I made a coffee and sat at the kitchen table with it. I sat and thought. Who — and what had they wanted?

There was no obvious candidate. The only people giving me trouble recently had been the Geordies, and this wasn't their style. Subtle they were not.

Someone from the more distant past, then? No-one came to mind.

Whoever it was, what had they wanted? There was nothing here worth looting. Activity on the computer suggested it was

85

information they had been after. But what?

It was a mystery. I shook my head and gave up. But I had been alerted. Now I would have to wait and see if anything else happened.

★ ★ ★

I found it too quiet in the cottage after that. I wasn't in the mood for solitude. So I went across to see Jimmy Mack. He was in the doorway of his shed, mending lobster pots. I sometimes wonder if I should get some lobster pots myself. Mending them seems good therapy. Jimmy does it all the time.

'Any more bodies?' he asked, scarcely looking up.

'Not today, Jim. You seen any?'

He shook his head. 'Not a one.'

I sat down on a log stump, a big piece of driftwood that somebody strong had once lugged up from the beach.

'It can be a wild place, the South Gare,' Jimmy reflected.

'It certainly was the other day.'

I watched his thick, old fingers manipulate the cord and tie the knots. It was a wonder he could still do it, with his bad eyesight and his arthritis. He was on automatic, I suppose. He'd been doing this all his life.

'Have you still got any contacts down there, Jim?'

'At the Gare?' He nodded. 'A few. Fellas that have been there donkeys' years.'

I knew the fishermen's huts passed down the generations, prized assets for working men to go to on their days off for a bit of fishing, or just to sit and talk about the old days, when you could walk across the Tees estuary on the backs of salmon and porpoises. The huts were an alternative to sheds, greenhouses and pigeon crees on allotments.

I didn't tell him about Nancy Peters. He would probably have been outraged. So far as I knew, the traditional embargo on women staying overnight in the huts still existed. So one of the huts actually being in female ownership would certainly have set him off.

'Have you heard anything recently?' I asked.

'From down there?'

I nodded and yawned, resigned to having to be patient.

Still without looking up, he said with satisfaction, 'There's hell on at the minute.'

'How's that?'

For a man who never left the house now — in his own estimation, at least — he knew an awful lot about what was going on over a surprisingly wide area.

'Rumours, and more rumours. Things, bad things, are going to happen, they say.'

'Like what?'

He cut through a cord and dropped the knife he was using. Then he pushed the creel off his knees, mended. Finally, he looked up at me.

'You want to keep out of it,' he said flatly.

I chuckled. 'It's a bit late for that, Jim. What are you hearing?'

'There's trouble brewing.'

He picked up the knife again and pared a fingernail that had become a bit jagged.

'There's always trouble, Jim. Wherever there's people, you can't avoid it.'

He pointed the knife at me and said, 'Don't you go talking down to me, young man. I may not have your education, but . . . '

'You don't. You're right there. You got out of school when you were fifteen. I had to wait till I was sixteen.'

It took a moment, but then he grinned.

'So what are you on about?' I asked.

He sighed and stuck the knife into the ground.

'There's talk of some foreign company taking over the port and the river. They want to do all sorts of things, apparently. Getting rid of the fishermen's huts is just one of them.'

'How can they do that?'

'By not renewing the lease on the land. That's what folk say.'

'The huts have been there a long time, haven't they?'

'Forever, nearly. Longer than I've been here, anyway. But the land they're on is leased. Originally from Lord Zetland. Then the Tees Conservancy Commission. I don't know for sure who owns it now.'

The private-sector company that ran the port, presumably, I thought. Or the owners of the nearby steelworks. But the huts were an institution, as was Paddy's Hole where the boats were kept. Surely nobody would do away with them?

Yet, as soon as I framed the question, I knew that it was possible. Of course it was. Anything was possible now the world was run by accountants, and cutting costs and making money was all that counted.

It was the problem Nancy Peters had mentioned, and probably the reason she had come into contact with James Campbell.

'There were fishermen there,' Jimmy continued, 'even before the South Gare was built. It's not right.'

All this somehow had to be down to PortPlus. So far as I knew, no other foreign company had appeared on the scene. Besides,

Nancy had said it was them. Jack Gregory had hinted at it, too. It had to be them.

'That's not all, either,' Jimmy said darkly.

I looked at him.

'There's talk of them wanting to build another nuclear power station on what's left of the dunes this side of the river. On the other side they want to do away with the Seal Sands nature reserve, and put some of them wind generators there. All to make money,' he added, looking round for somewhere to spit.

I wondered if it could be done, all that, and again knew the answer as soon as I'd asked the question. Once someone said 'new jobs', all obstacles fell away instantly, especially when there was a downturn in the economy and politicians' eyes were on the next election.

God help the seals on what was left of Seal Sands, I thought, if that was what PortPlus had in mind. Not to mention the fishermen at the South Gare — and probably a few other innocent bystanders, as well.

'Anything else?' I asked almost with dread.

'That's enough, isn't it?'

I nodded. It was. For now.

'They'll likely cut off access to the South Gare altogether,' Jimmy added with a sort of grim satisfaction. 'By Tod Point, probably, just like it used to be.'

He was thinking of a time before the river improvements were made, and the Tees emptied into the sea by a vast delta that stretched from Hartlepool to the edge of Coatham and Redcar.

'They can't do that,' I said dubiously. 'What about the steelworks?'

'How long is that going to last?'

I grimaced. You had to wonder. Redcar Steelworks was all that was left of the steel industry on Teesside. It wasn't much.

'The wind's getting up,' Jimmy said, pausing to stare past me at the darkening sky, as if that were another harbinger of calamity.

'James Campbell,' I said with a weary sigh. 'Do you know anything about his involvement in all this?'

Why not ask? I thought. Jimmy seemed to know about everything else.

'I know the fishermen's association had asked him to look into this takeover. I wouldn't be surprised if the people interested in wild birds and seals, and whatnot, hadn't asked him as well.'

I wouldn't have been surprised either. It sounded as if PortPlus had stirred up a hornet's nest down there. Poor old James Campbell, as the local MP, must have been run off his feet.

Soon afterwards I left Jimmy to it. He had

91

given me a lot more to think about, but I almost wished I hadn't bothered going to see him — or listened to Jack Gregory and Nancy Peters either. Until I'd started talking to them, I'd had a good job in prospect.

★ ★ ★

I groaned when I saw Bill Peart's vehicle coming back along the track. I was in a want-to-be-alone mood by then.

'The sea has calmed down a bit,' Bill said as he announced himself.

I nodded without much interest. 'I'm going to have a beer, Bill. Fancy one?'

'Why not?' he said, looking at his watch. 'I'm off duty now.'

'You're kidding!' I chuckled. 'Since when have you started knocking off work this early? Have they done away with overtime payments?'

He made a face and settled himself in a comfortable chair near the stove. It looked like he was here for a while.

I opened a couple of bottles of Newcastle Brown Ale, handed him one and flopped onto the sofa with another.

He inspected the bottle carefully. 'I thought they'd stopped making this stuff?'

'In Newcastle, they did. But it's still made

somewhere. Nottingham, maybe.'

'The modern world, eh?' he said with a sigh. 'I wonder if you could put your finger on when it stopped making sense.'

'Just before you were born, probably.'

He grinned.

'So how's it going, Bill?'

'Nowhere fast. We know how Campbell died and where his body was found, but not much else. No-one seems to know why he was at the South Gare, and there are lots of possibilities when it comes to who might have killed him.'

'He was a busy man,' I said. 'Plenty of friends, and just as many enemies, probably.'

'That's about right. I suppose it was worth it? His lifestyle, I mean.'

I shook my head. I wasn't getting into that. I hadn't had enough to drink. Besides, I was tired. I just wanted the day to end soon.

'How's Jac?'

'All right, I think. She's gone away for a bit.'

'Sensible girl. We don't want her caught up in this.'

That, at least, I could agree with.

'What's happening about that job you mentioned?'

'I'm not sure, Bill. I talked to the CEO, and I met the chairman of the company. The contract is mine if I want it. The trouble is I'm not sure I want it now. I've talked to a few people since then, and they've told me things I didn't like to hear. It's a company that seems to be upsetting an awful lot of people.'

'Who is it?'

'They call themselves PortPlus. They may be an American outfit, although I'm not sure about that. Anyway, they're making a takeover bid for Teesport.'

'Really?' He whistled. 'That's going to be big news.'

I nodded.

'They're talking about big investment in the area and making the port operation more efficient. Presumably that will result in new jobs, but it's also going to threaten the fishermen at the Gare and various environmental interests.'

'What's your problem?'

I grimaced. 'Frankly? I didn't care for their chief executive, and I do like some of the people opposed to what they plan to do. James Campbell was opposed to them, as well,' I added for good measure. 'At first, according to his agent, he was supportive. Then he changed his mind and was about to start campaigning to get them stopped. Instead, it was him that got stopped.'

In the sudden silence we stared at one other, Bill seemingly as startled by the implications of my throwaway remark as I was myself.

'Well, now,' he murmured thoughtfully. 'Isn't that interesting?'

'Isn't it?' I agreed, wondering why I hadn't thought of it earlier.

Then I went to find a couple more bottles of Newcastle Brown Ale.

17

A lot of work was done in the nineteenth century to make the Tees a more navigable river. As well as building staiths and docks, and developing the new towns of Middlesbrough and West Hartlepool, the coal owners and the ironmasters created the Tees Conservancy Commission and charged it with improving the river for shipping. The TCC dredged deeper channels, built miles of retaining walls and also built both the North Gare and the South Gare breakwaters to improve the entrance to the river. Most of these structures were made of slag, the waste from the new blast furnaces.

The TCC did a good job, good enough to suffice for well over a hundred years. Then in the 1980s the government of the day started hunting for things to privatize. One of the things they found was Teesport and, in effect, the role of the TCC. Control of the river, the port and much associated land passed from public to private control. After that, a succession of ownership changes had led up to where we were now.

Now, it seemed, some sort of American

collective investment fund — or whatever PortPlus was — was looking to take everything over, and do away with the fishermen's huts, the seals and much else besides. Once they had made their money, the way these things worked, they would no doubt soon be away again, leaving a bitter legacy. The new jobs would turn out to be fewer and less permanent than hoped, and the area would be changed forever, not necessarily for the better. It didn't seem good enough.

It was time I gave PortPlus my answer to the question they had put to me.

★ ★ ★

I met Mike Rogers in his office.

'Frank! Good to see you again. How are you?'

I smiled my answer. Then I declined the offer of coffee but sat down at the guest coffee table with him.

'So what do you think?' he asked. 'Going to take up our offer?'

'I have a few questions first, Mike. I was wondering what plans PortPlus have for the area around the lower reaches of the Tees.'

'Where are you thinking of, exactly?' he asked with a puzzled frown.

'The undeveloped part of Seal Sands on the north side, say, and around the South Gare, south of the river.'

'Plans?' He looked dubious now. 'No plans, Frank. We haven't even got hold of the business yet. How could we have plans?'

That sounded pretty naïve to me, given the scale of the investment they were contemplating. No plans? Come on!

'A wish list, then. What do you want to do down there? I gather there's some controversy building with the locals.'

'Locals? There's no-one lives there, Frank.'

'The fishermen, for example, and various environmental groups.'

'Oh, I see.' He nodded and his expression became grim. 'Do I gather you've been talking to people?'

'I have. I need to know what I'm getting into.'

He looked down and studied his hands for a moment while he worked out what he wanted to say.

'We are considering various options for land both sides of the river. As a responsible, well-run company we would naturally want to maximize the return from our investment. Yes?'

It was a corporate speech, the kind of stuff someone like him would deliver routinely at press conferences. I could tell he was unhappy with the way the conversation was going. Me asking questions, and talking to people, was not what he had wanted.

'Then there's the local Member of Parliament, James Campbell,' I said, undeterred. 'Or there was. He's dead now, murdered. I'm wondering how he fitted into the situation.'

Rogers shook his head impatiently.

'Frank, let me be blunt. We're intent on moving quickly on our acquisition proposal. We asked you to undertake an overview of security issues and develop an outline strategy. For that we would pay you a handsome fee. Either you can do that for us, or you can't. And I'm bound to tell you, Frank, I'm getting negative vibes from your attitude and the questions you are throwing at me. Now,' he said, fixing me with a piercing look, 'are you in or out? With us, or not?'

'Not,' I said, getting to my feet. 'I'll show myself out.'

★ ★ ★

After I left the PortPlus office, I went to see a guy I know who has been making a living as an independent forensic accountant for a few

99

years. His office was in the centre of the town, not far from the town hall.

'Frank Doy!' he said with a grin. 'Boy, you're looking good. Life must be sweet. Business booming?'

'It's not bad, Henry. All I need is a bit more cash. A lot more, actually.'

'So you want me to find you some?'

'Wouldn't that be nice? No, I've come to invite you out for lunch. Yes, you're right,' I added, anticipating his next question. 'I do want something from you in return.'

He chuckled with delight and shook his head. 'I saw that one coming! What do you want?'

'I want to pick your brains about takeovers, especially hostile takeovers.'

He raised an eyebrow. 'What sector are we talking about here?'

'Ports, basically, and everything to do with them. Shipping, industrial land development — all of that.'

'What's in it for me?'

'My company for an hour or so, and a pork pie and a pint.'

Henry scratched his bald head and pushed back his glasses, which had worked their way down his nose. 'Sounds good,' he said after a moment's thought. 'C'mon! Let's go.'

Henry steered me to the Blast Furnace, a pub in the old Middlesbrough tradition, a place where a lot of serious drinking was done. It was heaving. Our entry was no more noticed than it would have been on the terraces of old Ayresome Park, half-way through a derby against Sunderland. There was lots of terse conversation, and lots of eyes glued on the horse racing being broadcast on the many televisions dotted around the big room.

Henry sighed with satisfaction and smiled at me. 'Who says pubs are dying?'

'The only thing missing from the old days is the cigarette smoke,' I said agreeably.

'Ah, well. You can't have everything.'

We got what we wanted from the bar and found seats in a comparatively quiet corner. It wasn't my idea of a secluded watering hole, but it seemed to be Henry's.

'So what are you up to?' he asked me.

'Not a lot. A potential client asked me to do a job for them. I'd never heard of them, and what I've discovered since has not impressed me. I want to know what they're doing.'

Henry nodded and sipped his beer. 'Takeovers, eh?'

'Takeovers. These pies any good?' I asked,

scrutinizing the paper-wrapped packages we had picked up at the bar.

'The best. They get them from the old Newbould's place.'

The legendary Middlesbrough pork butcher. I raised my eyebrows with approval and unwrapped one of the pies.

'I don't care for salad,' Henry confided, following suit, 'and foreign muck like that.'

'No, of course not.' I nodded. 'So you come here?'

'Most days.'

It was a wonder he was still with us. Henry had never enjoyed the best of health, and he carried on in the same old way with fags, beer and pork pies as he always had done. It was as if the twenty-first century had yet to arrive.

But he was good at what he did for a living, very good, and I wasn't going to be the one who criticized his lifestyle.

'Hostile takeovers,' he said thoughtfully. 'How hostile?'

'I'm not sure,' I admitted.

'Well, it's pretty straightforward. If the board of the target company says no to a proposed offer, and the predator company continues anyway, it's a hostile takeover. The predator then makes a public offer for shares or simply starts buying them on the open market. Sometimes they try to make things easier for themselves by engineering a change of management, and getting a more sympathetic board.'

I nodded, as if I knew all this. 'And after that it's a matter of which side has the strongest will, and how much the prospective buyer wants to spend?'

'That's about right.'

How much money, I wondered, did PortPlus have and want to spend?

'Ports, you said?' Henry mused. 'Not Teesport?'

'That's the one.'

'So who are we talking about?'

I hesitated briefly but there was no point in concealment now I'd come this far.

'An outfit called PortPlus. Probably American, although I'm not certain.'

Henry's face screwed up with thought. 'I wish you could still smoke in here,' he said.

'We could go outside?'

He shook his head. 'I'll manage.'

I was relieved about that. No way did I want to go through the embarrassing smokers' ritual of standing outside the door, racing through a cigarette fast in order to get back inside before the beer went flat or somebody nicked it.

'I've not heard of them,' Henry said. 'Can you give me any names?'

I mentioned Rogers and McCardle. Henry hadn't heard of them either.

'I'll do some checking when I get back to the office,' he said, 'but I can tell you now I'm puzzled.'

'Why's that?'

'Usually you hear things when a takeover is being mooted, or an offer being prepared, but I've heard nothing about this one. I do some work for the Teesport people, and I haven't heard anything from them either. They're certainly not running scared.'

He looked at me. 'How far do you want me to go with this, Frank? I can give you a couple of hours gratis. After that I'll have to start charging.'

'Of course. Don't go to the ends of the earth, Henry, but I need to know what's going on. I'm not asking you to do it for nothing.'

'Fair enough.' He nodded. 'Come on, then. Drink up! The sooner we get back, the sooner I can get started.'

18

After leaving Henry, I drove home slowly. I needed to clear my head of all the rubbish I'd collected over the past few days. I wasn't thinking straight. Things were happening that I couldn't get my head round.

Could PortPlus really be behind what had happened to James Campbell? Bill Peart and I had managed to persuade ourselves that they might be. They certainly had the motive. Campbell had been about to launch a campaign against them, and big bucks were at stake. Very big. I had no idea what a takeover of Teesport would cost, but you had to be talking hundreds of millions. Sterling, too, not dollars.

I had begun to wonder as well, if the threats I had experienced had come from PortPlus. The job offer could have been an attempt to get me onside, and stop me making trouble. Perhaps that had been the carrot, and the various warnings, the stick?

That made sense, of a kind. The problem with it was that it made PortPlus out to be more of an organized crime syndicate than a straightforward investment vehicle. Perhaps that was what they were?

I needed to do more research on them. I couldn't leave it all to Henry.

★ ★ ★

I got to work on the computer, but I didn't get very far. Heavy knocking on the door interrupted me after half an hour or so. Jimmy Mack again, I thought with a weary smile. No doubt wanting more liquid refreshment, and to download more gloom and doom.

But when I opened the door I had a brief moment to register surprise before a hand grabbed my shirt front and pulled me down the steps. I sprawled face-down and tried to curl up as the kicking began. I was soon in agony and retching for breath. Caught cold, there was nothing I could do but endure and hope to survive.

Eventually it stopped. Someone spoke to me. A deep, hard voice, with words I couldn't decipher until someone threw ice-cold water over my head.

'You were warned,' the voice said. 'But clever bugger that you are, you thought you knew better!'

I opened one eye cautiously and saw a blurred image of someone leaning over me.

106

The voice seemed vaguely familiar. I tried to focus, but it was no good. I blacked out.

More cold water. I gagged and vomited, and gasped for air. Then my insides caught fire. The pain dragged me back closer to the surface.

I identified the voice of my tormentor. Geordie-speak. He was still there, towering above me. I sensed others were there too, looking on, but they were indistinct shapes. I concentrated on the voice.

'D'you hear me, Doy?'

I raised my face slightly from the ground and vomited a mess of blood and mucus. My head felt split open. I let it fall back to the ground again.

'You were told! Stay away from the cops, we told you. And stop poking around in things that don't concern you. Then what do you do? You get all cosy with that cop mate of yours!'

I stayed still and kept my eyes shut.

'For the moment,' he went on in a calmer tone, sounding almost reasonable, 'you've got protection. But it won't always be like that. If we have to come back here again, you'll not live to tell the tale, sunshine. You'll be over that fucking cliff!'

It wasn't a good time to be arguing. In fact, it wasn't a good time to be doing anything.

Even lying still hurt like hell.

Later, I wondered who it was that was supposed to be affording me protection. Whoever it was, they hadn't done much of a job. I was damned lucky I hadn't ended up the same way as James Campbell.

★ ★ ★

Eventually I realized that no-one had spoken for a while. I certainly hadn't, and when I thought about it I didn't believe anyone else had either. I opened an eye again and cautiously raised my head an inch or two. The pain was intense. I grimaced and ground my teeth together. But, so far as I could see, I was alone.

All I wanted to do was lie there until the hurting stopped but some residue of sense persuaded me that wouldn't be a good idea. The night was coming on and it was getting colder. I started gearing up mentally, and then I started moving. Slowly. In time, I got to my knees, and finally on to my feet. Then began the long struggle to get back inside the house.

I managed. Somehow. Later, a lot later, a hot shower helped, as did a glass of the whisky I kept mostly for Jimmy Mack's benefit.

I avoided mirrors but I started reluctantly making an inventory of the damage sustained. Probable concussion. Probable cracked ribs.

But otherwise mostly bruises, cuts, scrapes, strains and tears. And damaged pride, and plenty of self-loathing for allowing myself to get suckered like that.

These people were serious, I had to admit. I had taken them too lightly. I held myself together and counted the cost of my mistake. It could have been worse, I told myself. I could easily have been dead.

Most things would heal themselves in time. The cuts and bruises. The concussion would go, with rest. If the ribs were cracked there was nothing to be done but endure the pain, with the help of whatever medication I could find — more whisky, probably. As for the rest of it — the hurt pride and mounting anger — well, I would look forward to a return engagement. And I would make damn sure there was one.

The only other thought that came to me was that people who went in for this sort of thing were not likely to be the same ones who had tip-toed through my house trying not to leave a trace. That must have been somebody else.

★ ★ ★

I didn't get a lot of sleep that night. Waves of pain kept me awake. There was plenty of time to mull things over and dream dreams of revenge. Sometime in the long, dark hours, I acknowledged that some sort of protection really must have been thrown over me. Otherwise I wouldn't have survived.

The Geordies were worried about me, and what I had seen at the South Gare. They had made that plain enough several times. So something had held them back from giving me a bullet in the head.

I wondered if that protection would still apply now that I had turned down PortPlus. I couldn't think of anyone else who might have told the Geordies to hold back. The restraining order might well be lifted now. It was a sobering thought.

Metaphorically, I shook my head, while careful to minimize actual movement. It seemed too fanciful. All I could really be sure of was that I was able to identify the men who had probably murdered James Campbell. It all came back to that, and that alone.

To get anywhere, I knew I still needed to know more about the dead man, as well as about PortPlus. Easier said than done, but I did know one place where I might learn more. As soon as I could move and see properly again I would go there. That was the plan; it wasn't much of one, but it helped me get through the night.

19

There were about fifty fishermen's huts at the South Gare, all of them painted green, as required initially by Lord Zetland and now by custom and tradition. They weren't actually identical, but they were all out of the same toy box: sloping or pitched roof, shuttered windows, tin smoke stack — and green. I picked one with wood smoke coming from the flue to make my first inquiry.

A couple of elderly gents were occupying condemned armchairs just inside the open door, a pot-bellied stove going like a blast furnace behind them. I made sure my Canadian logger's hat was in place before I approached them. With the big peak and the ear-flaps, I hoped it would at least partially hide my battle scars.

'The Peters hut?' the one with glasses said, peering hard at me.

I nodded.

'Never heard of it. Have you, Jack?'

'Heard of what?'

'He's looking for a bloke called Peters,' Glasses said in a louder voice.

'Nobody here with that name,' Jack said, shaking his head.

By then, I was beginning to wonder if fishermen can get Alzheimer's, like the rest of us. Maybe even earlier, despite all the oily fish they eat.

'A young woman,' I said a little desperately. 'Called Nancy.'

'Nancy? Oh, aye!' Glasses said. 'You should have said that was who you wanted. Nancy. End of the back row, there. I think she's in just now.

'Been in a car crash, have you?' he added with a chuckle.

So the disguise wasn't all that good.

'I fell out of my pram when I was a baby,' I said through gritted teeth.

At least it made him laugh.

As I turned away, I heard his mate say, 'Looking for somebody, was he?'

'A woman.'

'A woman? Here? He'll be lucky!'

I grinned and kept going.

Only one cabin in the back row had smoke puffing from the chimney. Hoping that was the one, I tapped on the door.

Chair legs scraped on a wooden floor. The door handle squeaked. Then the door began to ease open. It stopped and I heard a woman's voice cursing as she dealt with some

problem or other. An obstruction, it seemed.
I gave a wry smile, recognizing the voice. It
was the right hut.

The door finally swung open to reveal
Nancy Peters.

'Oh!' she said with alarm. 'It's you.'

Overcoming her initial shock, she peered
closer and winced. 'What happened?'

'It's a long story,' I said with a grimace.

'Well, what do you want?' she demanded,
no doubt still sour about my connection to
PortPlus.

'I'd like to talk to you.'

'What about?'

'James Campbell. Something's come up.'

She hesitated and then said, 'You'd better
come in.'

She stepped back and I moved forward.

The hut was small, no more than a single
room about ten or twelve feet square, plus a
built-on, cupboard-size extension that probably contained a portable loo of some sort.
Within its strict limitations, it was surprisingly
comfortable and homely. I gazed around with
interest at the pine-clad walls, taking in the
bric-a-brac on little shelves and the flowery
curtains at the only window. The feminine
touch. It wasn't much in evidence in Jimmy
Mack's hut on the beach below Risky Point.

'I've never been in one of these before,

Nancy. It's very nice. Are they all the same?'

'Pretty much. You'd better sit down. You're using up too much valuable space.'

I sat down awkwardly on one of the two chairs around the kitchen table, trying not to breathe or place pressure on any part of me.

'You live here full-time?' I asked, concentrating on conducting myself as if I wasn't coming apart at the seams.

She shrugged. 'Put it this way. I don't have any other place to live.'

'I thought women . . . '

'We're not,' she said quickly. 'Women aren't even allowed here overnight, which is an anachronistic male legacy from feudal times.'

'So?'

'Most of them knew my grandad. So they turn a blind eye.'

'An eye like mine,' I said, closing my good eye and squinting at her through the other one.

'Who did that to you? Let me guess,' she added with sudden inspiration. 'PortPlus — or their agents?'

I nodded, and immediately regretted the movement as pain shot across my face and down my neck.

'I think so,' I admitted. 'The people who probably killed James anyway.'

'That why you wanted to talk to me again?

114

It was PortPlus, wasn't it?'

This time I didn't nod. I didn't say anything either. She knew the answer to her question as well as I did. PortPlus. It had to be something to do with them.

'We both want the same thing,' I said instead. 'James Campbell's killers. Right?'

Now it was her turn to nod agreement.

'Then let's work together,' I suggested.

★　★　★

Nancy made a pot of tea, boiling the kettle on an ancient cast-iron stove that was throwing out a gentle heat.

'I see you're burning driftwood?'

'Oh, yes!' she said with a smile. 'There's nothing better.'

'And sea coal?'

'That, too. I like free stuff.'

I nodded with approval. 'I do the same,' I told her.

'Where do you live?'

'Risky Point, on the coast just south of Boulby.'

'Really? Does it get cold down there?'

'Just a bit. Windy, mostly.'

She nodded. 'Like here, then. I need the heat. I spent too many years in Africa.'

I had wondered about her accent, without

115

being able to place it.

'What were you doing there?'

She poured two mugs of tea before she answered. Handing one to me, she said, 'I was born there. Zimbabwe. They used to call it Southern Rhodesia.'

'A long time ago.'

'That's right. It was.' She nodded. 'James was from Africa, too.'

'Born there?'

She nodded again.

'I didn't know that.'

'Well, he didn't advertise the fact.' She shrugged and added, 'I suppose we were both refugees, of a sort.'

The information volunteered encouraged me to probe for more.

'You said you believed James had been murdered, even before I told you he was. What made you so sure?'

'He was a serious nuisance to certain people — PortPlus, in particular. Your employers,' she added for emphasis.

'Because he was campaigning against what they wanted to do?'

'Exactly.'

She held her mug up to her face and sipped her tea thoughtfully.

I wondered if it could really be that simple. You don't usually murder someone just

116

because they don't agree with you. But maybe these people were different? And there was big money involved, I reminded myself yet again. That always makes a difference.

'They never were my employers,' I corrected her. 'I'm a freelance consultant. I was considering an offer they had made to me.'

'Whatever,' she said with a shrug.

'Not that it matters now anyway. I've turned their offer down.'

She looked at me with fresh interest. But I steered the conversation away from me.

'Murdering James seems a bit drastic, don't you think? He was an MP doing his job, after all. Why didn't they just hire an expensive PR firm to argue their case in public with him?'

She laughed scornfully. 'You'll have to ask them that!' Then she looked at me with a frown. 'What made you turn them down?'

'The job was beginning to seem very uncongenial,' I said with a rueful smile, 'something to steer clear of. I didn't know anything about PortPlus, and I was having difficulty finding anything. Where does their money come from, for instance? Do they actually have any, if it comes to that? And what experience do they have of running port operations? Besides, I like this place — and the rest of the riverside. I wasn't sure I wanted to see another nuclear power station

117

built here — or the fishermen moved off either.'

Nancy laughed. 'You told them all that? You're lucky you didn't get a bullet in the back of the head!'

'Yes,' I admitted. 'I've thought that myself. Instead, this happened,' I added, raising my hands to my face.

She got up and leaned towards me. 'Let me have a look at those cuts on your . . .'

I jerked away. She pulled back from whatever she was about to do.

'What's wrong?'

'Sorry.' I grimaced and pointed to my side, where she had brushed against me. 'There's some damage there, as well.'

'Your ribs? How bad is it?'

'I've had worse.'

'Really? Some life you lead!'

She held back a moment longer. Then she shook her head and got on with it.

She brought a bowl of warm water to the table and added some drops of disinfectant. Careful to avoid pressing against my side, she began dabbing gently at my face with a pad of cotton wool.

'What are you — a nurse?'

She just grunted, and continued dabbing.

'I've already done that,' I told her between gritted teeth.

'There's still some bleeding.'

I let her continue. I could do with some tlc. Besides, I liked her being near. Her scent was warm and pleasant, her body soft and promising. Without the eminently sensible duffel coat, she was a major attraction.

Just then, though, my injuries were of greater concern. Healing would have to take its course, but I was ready to accept any help on offer to speed the process. Making my face more presentable would be a good start. After that, I would have to hope the ribs were bruised rather than cracked. I would find that out in the next couple of days. Either the pain would ease off or it would stay the same, and quite possibly get worse.

'I don't suppose you would consider going to a hospital and having an X-ray?'

'No. I haven't got time.'

She chuckled. 'Tough guy, huh?'

'That's me.'

'Let's hope it lasts.'

That smarted. I suddenly wanted her to take me seriously, and believe in me.

'They're not going to get away with it,' I said firmly.

'That's good to know.'

Maybe she believed me; maybe she didn't. It didn't matter. I believed me. I had an Old Testament attitude to things like this.

Someone was going to be sorry.

'What brought you all the way from Zimbabwe to here?' I asked, moving on.

'Poverty, basically,' she said with a wry chuckle.

'You could have chosen a better solution.'

'Possibly.' She stopped what she was doing and peered closely for a moment. 'There! That will have to do. I don't think there's anything more I can do. You don't need stitching, not on your face. And you'll just have to put up with the bruising and the lacerations for a while.'

'Thank you — Doctor!'

She smiled and sat back down.

'We lost the farm where I grew up,' she said. 'Mugabe's gangsters took it at gunpoint. My father was murdered, and Mum didn't live long after that. I was all alone then, and the future I'd been preparing for all my life was gone. So I came back to England to look up my grandfather, my dad's father. But I was too late. He'd gone, too.'

She looked around and added, 'He left me this place and his Whitby coble. I was very grateful.'

And then she had met James Campbell. Poor kid!

'Was James from Zimbabwe, too?'

'Well, he lived there, growing up, but he

was born in South Africa.'

She added, 'He didn't like to talk about all that too much. His life was here now, he used to say, and he was determined to make the best of it.'

And so he had. Until his luck ran out. Poor sod!

PortPlus wouldn't have liked the idea of Campbell leading the campaign against them. He was a dangerous opponent. I wondered if they had weighed things up and decided to get rid of him. Not the conventional way to do business, but it happens. Usually, though, in countries like Russia or Mexico.

But it was all supposition. I had no evidence for it. Not yet, anyway.

The answers I needed were not here, and I had troubled Nancy far too much already.

'I'd better be going,' I said. 'I've taken enough of your time.'

She shrugged. 'Time is something I have plenty of.'

I levered myself to my feet carefully, not wanting anything to fall off my fragile frame.

'Where are you going?' she asked.

'Home.'

'Really? And do you think you'll make it?'

'I don't see why not.'

'Driving will be hard with busted ribs.'

'I got here, didn't I?'

'That was then. This is now.'

She was right. I was stiffening up. The knowledge didn't make me feel any better. But if I could make it back to the Land Rover, a hundred yards or so away, I should be all right. I would just swallow the pain and drive — and hope for the best.

'Stay here tonight,' she said.

I smiled wryly.

'I mean it,' she said sharply. 'You're in no fit state to be driving.'

The arguments I was about to use suddenly all dried up. She was right. I was kidding myself. I might well pass out on the road, and if that happened I probably wouldn't be the only victim. Time to get real.

'Where would I . . . ?'

I glanced around helplessly.

'We'll manage,' Nancy said firmly. 'I've got some pain-killers you could take — but not if you're going to drive.'

I shrugged and sat back down like an old man. There are times when you just have to concede the point.

20

'So you can't do without us, eh?' the thin, wiry man with short fair hair said. 'It's going to cost you, us coming back all this way.'

'Who is it, anyway?' his partner, tall and dark-haired, asked.

The boss looked at the man in the suit and invited him to pick up the conversation.

'The man was a witness to the . . . the disposal of the body. We've tried to buy him off, and failed. We've also tried intimidation, and that didn't work either.'

'So he's got to go?'

The man in the suit nodded. 'We believe so.'

'You referred to 'the man',' the partner pointed out. 'That implies there is more than one target.'

'Yes. There's a woman, as well.'

'They are together?'

'Separate.'

'Why do you . . . ?'

'Just do it,' the boss said, coming in heavily. 'Do it, and we'll pay the going rate. OK?'

'Sure,' said the thin, wiry man with an easy smile. 'That's why we're here. We don't like the idea of witnesses any more than you do.'

21

Somehow we managed. Nancy produced an airbed and a quilt for me. They went on the bottom bunk, and I managed to lever myself on to it and lie down. Nancy went on the top bunk. The painkillers she administered did everything else. I took them, against my normal practice, because I knew I needed to get some sleep. They worked.

The next morning, surprisingly, I felt a bit better. I even managed to sit up.

'You've passed the first test,' an amused voice said from the top bunk.

I slowly got to my feet. 'Been awake long, yourself?'

She shook her head and yawned. Then she swept a cascade of hair away from her face. 'I'm not an early-morning fisherman,' she said. 'Later on suits me better.'

She looked wonderful, skin glowing, hair all over her face, coming to terms with the start of a new day. I would have given a lot to look as healthy as she did.

'Got to get started,' I said, reluctantly making some gentle stretching movements.

'Right! Let's do it. Breakfast?'

'That would be good.'

Breakfast wasn't up to much, but I didn't complain. The coffee and the toast she served up helped get me ready for the day.

'What are you going to do now?' Nancy asked as we ate.

I hesitated, and then I told her. Why not? She was on my side, wasn't she? Or I was on hers. I wasn't sure which it was, but in practical terms it came to the same thing.

I had decided to visit Henry again. Getting beaten up had injected even more urgency into my enquiries. I needed to know more about what I was up against.

'Right. I'll come with you,' Nancy announced when I told her.

'I don't think so,' I said firmly. 'This isn't your fight.'

'Not my . . . ?' She powered into highly-indignant mode. It was impressive to see. 'Now look here, Frank! I'm not too bothered about what happened to you, but I intend seeing justice done for James. Where you go today, I go. All right? Besides,' she added, turning it down a bit, 'you're in no condition to drive.'

I believed she was wrong there, but I wasn't entirely sure. I still suspected concussion. In fact, I was damned sure of it. I didn't want to pass out at the wheel and risk wiping out some passing innocent — as well as myself, of course.

'Can you drive a Land Rover?'

She looked at me scornfully. 'Are you serious? What on earth do you think I grew up driving, on the plains of Africa?'

I shook my head. 'I have no idea.'

'At age ten, I could nearly change a tyre all by myself. As a teenager I could fix most things that go wrong with a Land Rover engine. A Land Rover was all I ever drove until I moved to the big city!'

I gave up. Obviously she was coming with me, as driver — and mechanic.

'So a fishing boat's easy, with all that experience behind you?'

'Well,' she said, relenting, 'I'm not so good at the navigating or the fishing parts, but I can certainly cope with the boat's engine.'

'And there I was, the other day,' I said with a chuckle, 'thinking you were just a useless, hippy sort of woman.'

★　★　★

First, I phoned Bill Peart, to let him know the Geordies had been around again.

'No,' he said, in answer to my query, 'we haven't found them yet, and we don't know who they are.'

126

'The rental truck?'

'The company said it had been stolen.'

'A dead end, then.'

'So far.'

There wasn't anything else I could suggest.

'What happened this time?' he asked.

'It wasn't good, Bill. Three of them, and they jumped me. I got the worst of it. In fact, I never even laid a finger on any of them.'

I could tell he was surprised. It wasn't often I had to admit to being bested.

'How bad was it? How bad are you?'

'I'll be all right. Don't worry about it.'

'Sure?'

'Yeah.'

Just then, Nancy called out from the doorway to somebody passing by.

'Was that a woman's voice?' Bill asked suspiciously.

'Boy, I can see why they made you a detective!'

'I try to be helpful and sympathetic, and . . . '

'I know, I know. And all I can do is . . . Your concern is appreciated, Bill. Got to go now. I'll catch up with you later.'

★ ★ ★

We got to Middlesbrough mid-morning, and to Henry's office not long afterwards. First, I collected some money from a cash-point and treated us both to a bacon sandwich and a strong coffee in a little café round the corner from the town hall.

'My toast wasn't enough for you?' Nancy said sorrowfully. 'Or not to your liking?'

'It was excellent,' I assured her, 'but I feel the need for more sustenance before we meet Henry.'

'Oh?'

'We're likely to end up in a pub,' I told her. 'No good going there on an empty stomach.'

'Oh!' She looked happy to hear that.

'But I'm going to see Henry on my own first. I don't want him clamming up on me just because there's someone he doesn't know with me. We'll meet up afterwards. OK?'

She considered for a moment and then said, 'And you will tell me everything he says?'

'Of course.'

But I thought to myself: we'd have to see about that.

★ ★ ★

'Do for you?' Henry said over his shoulder in response to my gentle tap on his open door.

'You've started early, son. It's not even noon yet.'

'Oh, it's you,' he said without looking round.

Henry had a drink problem. He had always had one, which was possibly why he worked for himself rather than anyone else. Having said all that, drink rarely stopped him performing. He was good at what he did, very good, which was probably why he had no difficulty finding clients. They came looking for him, just as I had done — if you could count me as a client.

I sat down on the hard chair on the other side of his desk.

'Good Christ!' he said, looking up at last. 'What the fuck happened to you?'

'It's a long story.'

'Not something simple, like falling down the stairs after a couple too many, or being in a car crash?'

'Nothing like that,' I said, resisting the temptation to shake my head. 'Anyway, I'm recovering now.'

'That's good to hear.' Henry paused before adding with a frown, 'Anything to do with this inquiry?'

'It could be. I was told it was because I'm continuing to poke my nose into other people's business.'

'That right? You'd better not mention my name, then.'

'Wild horses wouldn't persuade me,' I said solemnly.

'No, of course they wouldn't.'

He turned the monitor he had been using away and pushed a few sheets of paper aside. Then he leaned forward, elbows on desk, and said, 'I'm puzzled, Frank.'

'Why's that?'

'So far as I can see,' Henry continued in steady, careful mode, 'PortPlus don't exist. At least, I can find nothing at all about them.'

I stared at him and shook my head.

'You're losing your touch, Henry. They exist, all right. I've been to their head office in Middlesbrough. I've met their CEO and chairman. They offered me work, for God's sake! Mind you,' I admitted, 'I couldn't find anything on them either.'

Henry just shrugged.

'They reckon they have port operations in the States,' I added.

'Well . . . '

A sharp knock on the door made Henry sit up and brought me wheeling round.

'Henry?' a voice said cautiously, as the door I had closed reopened.

'Ah!' Henry got up. 'I was hoping you'd be here, Kenny.'

The new arrival looked like one of Henry's drinking buddies. Burly, middle-aged, with a pug nose and a big face, he looked like a man who would soon be safely ensconced in the bar of the Blast Furnace. An old-school Middlesbrough man.

'Kenny, this is Frank Doy, an old pal. Come and sit down. We were just talking about this PortPlus business.'

I didn't like hearing that. I winced inwardly, wondering what confidential information Henry had revealed to a man I didn't know.

I got up and shook hands with Kenny Douglas. He studied me with sharp eyes and an amused smile. I realized quickly he was someone to take seriously, despite appearances.

'You're the private eye Henry was on about?' he growled. 'I'm pleased to meet you, Frank.'

'Kenny works for Teesport,' Henry said carefully. 'He's in a senior management position, with strategic financial responsibilities.'

I scolded myself for my doubts. I should have known better. Henry wouldn't divulge information lightly.

'I last looked like you do now,' Kenny said bluntly, 'when I got in a fight at the Royal Hotel in Port Clarence. Know it?'

I nodded. I did. Popular with steel erectors looking for cheap beds when construction was going on across the river, and quite likely closed now they'd all gone home. People didn't stay long on the north shore of the Tees if they could help it.

'They were tough blokes,' Kenny added. 'Far too good for me. I should have known better.'

'These guys jumped me,' I said rather lamely. 'I'm ashamed of myself, me being a private eye, and all.'

'Can happen to the best of us,' he said cheerfully.

He turned to Henry. 'Anything?'

Henry shook his head. 'I was just telling Frank they don't seem to exist. He disagrees.'

Kenny glanced at his watch. 'I haven't got a lot of time this morning. So I'll tell you quickly what I know.'

'About?' I ventured.

'Quite. We've heard the rumours, and the worries. We've had people coming to our door, demanding to know what's going on. The press are on to it. So we know all about what's supposed to be in the offing.

'But here's the rub. So far as we know, there's nothing to it. There's been no contact from a potential takeover bidder. Our shares are not doing anything unusual. So no-one is buying ready for a stealthy hostile bid. Nothing at all is happening. So far, it's just rumours.'

He looked back at Henry, who nodded and said, 'That's what I've been telling Frank.'

'Right,' Kenny said. 'I have to go. Nice meeting you, Frank. Let Henry know if you discover anything.'

He left, and Henry and I sat looking at each other, wondering where we went from here.

22

I wasn't best pleased when I got back to the Land Rover.

'Move over,' I said curtly. 'I'm driving.'

'Like that, is it?' Nancy said, staying put.

'Move over. I'm not in the mood for arguments.'

Her face set hard. 'Do I look like someone you can threaten? Do I look like a woman who will make way without a fight for a man with broken ribs and a sore head?'

I sighed and stood still for a moment, hanging on to the open door, wondering why I'd allowed her to come.

'I thought we were going to the Blast Furnace for lunch?' she pointed out.

'A pie and a pint, I'm sure I said.'

'Well, then? I like pies and pints.'

I slammed the door shut and shuffled round to the other side. There was no way I could drive. I could hardly stand up.

'Where to?' she asked after I'd got in.

'Just drive. I'll tell you where to turn.'

I was in a foul mood. So PortPlus didn't exist, didn't it? We'd see about that.

'What did Henry say?'

I grimaced but there was no way I could tell her. After all I'd said in praise of Henry and his skills as a forensic accountant, no way could I tell her he was useless, after all.

Bloody Henry! His buddy from Teesport was no better. To hell with both of them. A pair of drunks.

'Right at the crossroads,' I snapped. 'Then second left.'

'Over the border?'

'Where the border used to be. How do you know about that, anyway?'

She just grinned.

The other side of the railway. That was something else that didn't exist: the Border. Not now, anyway, and not for many years.

'Over the Border!', or north of the railway, used to be hell on earth according to legend. Not nowadays. The streets of terraced houses in what had been the poorest and toughest part of town had all been knocked down, and most of the pubs with them. Now the area where Middlesbrough had started life had a scatter of spanking new buildings amid the dereliction, like new shoots on a bomb site.

'So where are we going?' Nancy asked.

I had cooled down by then. So I gave her a civil answer.

'Henry and some bloke from Teesport told me PortPlus doesn't exist. For my own peace of mind — my sanity, actually — I'm going back to the PortPlus head office to prove they're wrong.'

'I'm with you,' Nancy said gravely.

I glanced sideways and saw the smile endangering her solemnity. My answering chuckle soon became a laugh. I couldn't help it.

'We'll show them!' I said, beginning to relax.

'Yessir! We surely will,' Nancy said, the very model of compliance.

★ ★ ★

It was a working day but there didn't seem to be a lot happening in the PortPlus offices. Mine was the only vehicle in the car park. The front door, when we reached it, was shut and locked. I could see no-one inside, in the reception area.

'They must be having a day off,' Nancy said, peering through the window.

'What, all of them?'

I took out my phone and rang Mike Rogers's number. No reply.

I moved off and started circling the building, my mind almost numb. Things didn't look good. In a bit of landscaped shrubbery I spotted a big board that, on inspection, turned out to be a for-sale-or-let hoarding. On automatic now, I pulled out my phone and punched in the number of the real estate office doing the advertising.

When my call was answered, I asked to be put through to whoever was handling Riverside House in Middlesbrough. A minute later I was speaking to a man who had drawn the short straw.

'PortPlus?' he said. 'I've never heard of them, I'm afraid.'

'Riverside House is their head office.'

'I'm sorry. That's not correct. Riverside House is a new-build property that we are trying to sell or lease. Can I ask what your interest is?'

'Look, I was inside the place a few days ago, at a meeting with their CEO and their chairman. But today the place is locked up and empty. What's going on?'

'Ah!' After a short pause, he continued. 'Last week was a bit special. The building was briefly occupied, but not by the company you mentioned. Let me see ... It was ... Enterprise Holdings. They leased it for a week for promotional purposes.'

'Are you sure?'

'Oh, yes! I let them in myself, and I let them out again at the end of the week. There's no mistake.'

Terrific! I thought grimly. They had certainly made a fool of me.

'Do you have a phone number and address for them?'

He did, and gave them to me. I made a note, without much confidence.

★ ★ ★

'What you got?' Nancy asked when I met up with her back in the car park.

I gave a bitter little laugh. 'Not much. They're no longer here. The people I met had hired the building for a week — supposedly for promotional purposes. Perhaps PortPlus really don't exist. Henry must be right.'

'Well, they used to exist,' Nancy said. 'I had a look in some rubbish bins round the back, and I found PortPlus stationery.'

I looked at the sample she was offering. Letterhead, envelopes, and other bits and pieces. I breathed again.

'So you weren't all wrong,' she said with a kindly smile. 'What now?'

'Hungry?'

She nodded.

'Then let's go and see Henry about that pie and pint.'

★ ★ ★

We found Henry exactly where I expected to find him — the same corner of the Blast Furnace he had been in yesterday, studying the racing form in some specialist rag.

'Get you one, Henry?'

He looked up. 'Frank! You're back.'

'You were right,' I said grimly. 'I don't think PortPlus does exist.'

'Ah!' He looked intrigued for a moment. Then he glanced questioningly at Nancy.

'She's with me,' I said quickly. 'Nancy, meet Henry.'

'With you?' Henry said, sounding surprised.

'We sleep together,' Nancy said.

'Really?'

Henry looked startled now, as well he might be — and as I was myself.

'Just once, actually,' Nancy added. 'In my hut.'

'In your hut?'

'What can I get you, Henry?' I asked desperately.

'The same as yesterday,' he said, sounding reluctant to be distracted from this new conversation.

'Nancy?'

'Whatever you're having, darling,' she said with a mischievous grin.

'Take no notice of her, Henry,' I said even more desperately.

'Oh, I won't!' he assured me, his eyes fixed with wonder on my modest companion.

I shook my head. I didn't know which of them was worse.

By the time I got back from the bar, they had already exchanged the basic information about PortPlus, and its non-existence.

'So where do we go from here?' Henry asked, eyes narrowing as he contemplated the difficulty of the road ahead. 'That guy McCardle, can you tell me anything about him?'

'Not much. In his fifties, I would say. Smooth operator. Strange accent — posh, but not home counties. Authoritative. Impressive.' I paused, having run out of suggestions.

'Try mining,' Nancy added quietly. 'And Africa.'

I looked at her with surprise. She gave me an apologetic shrug.

'Mining and Africa?' Henry said thoughtfully. 'That's interesting.'

Isn't it? I was thinking. Nancy, eh? What else did she know?

That was about it. We could get no further sitting in a pub. Henry needed to be back at his work console and on his computer. I just needed to be away, away from the noise and the people. My ribs were giving me gyp, and so was my head. I'd had enough for one day, even if it was still scarcely afternoon.

'If you've got any spare cash,' Henry said, waving his racing paper at me, 'put it on Moondancer in the four-thirty at Wetherby.'

'A dead cert?' I asked ironically.

'Just about!'

'Who's the trainer?' Nancy asked, as if she knew what she was talking about.

'Gordon Smith.'

'He's good,' I heard her say as I headed for the door.

That was the last thing I needed: a discussion about bloody race horse trainers!

★   ★   ★

'Where next, boss?'

'Home,' I said, without turning my head. 'I'll drop you off on the way.'

'No,' she said adamantly. 'You can't drive yet. I'll drive.'

'How are you going to get home?'

'I'm not. I'll stay with you.'

That stopped me in my tracks. I turned to look at her.

'I like you,' she said disarmingly. 'And I like what you're doing. You need help, and I want to help.'

I considered shouting at her, telling her to keep out of it. Then I realized I liked her too, and I really did need help. For a day or two even simple things like driving were going to be hard for me.

'I can't pay you,' I said gruffly. 'Bed and board only.'

'Sounds good,' she said cheerfully.

Perhaps it really did to someone in her position.

'There's plenty of hot water,' I added to encourage her, warming to the idea of a companion. 'And a bath, as well as a shower.'

'Mmm!'

'Know what?' I said, grinning. 'I'll be glad to have you along.'

'Now you're being soppy,' she said in admonishment.

But for a moment there, she held my hand in hers. I squeezed gently. Lordy, lordy! I thought. What are you doing, Frankie boy?

★   ★   ★

I knew what I was doing, all right. Thought I did, at least. I needed help for a day or two. Also, I wanted to pick Nancy's brains. It was obvious that she knew stuff I didn't.

'This is it,' I said as we left the road and pulled on to the rough track leading to Risky Point. 'Mine is the first cottage.'

'Whose is the other one?'

'It's Jimmy Mack's. He's an old fisherman, mostly retired now. You should get on well with him.'

She gave me a quick glance, to see if I was being sarcastic, taking her eyes off the road. Then she said, 'Oops!' as we hit a big pothole.

I clamped my teeth together and worked hard at ignoring the pain that had damn near convulsed me.

'Sorry about that,' Nancy said, throwing me another quick glance. 'I'll slow down.'

'Thanks,' I said through gritted teeth.

To her credit, she was very careful from then on, and we reached my parking spot without further incident.

'What a wonderful view!' Nancy exclaimed with delight. 'I'm staggered. I didn't know there was anywhere like this.'

'Not bad, is it?' I admitted.

'Oh, I can see why you live here!'

'Well, people either love it or hate it. If they shiver and go on about the cold wind and the isolation, I know which category they're in.'

'Huh! You want to send people like that to the South Gare. There's nowhere colder than that. The other cottage is a bit close to the edge of the cliff, though, isn't it?'

'Perilously close. They both are, and every year the edge gets a bit nearer.'

'Living dangerously, huh?' she said with a

grin. 'Life on the edge.'

'Exactly. Jimmy reckons I've got a bit more time, but it will be touch and go whether it's him or his cottage that goes first.'

'Make every day count,' she said gravely.

'That's the philosophy I try to keep in mind.'

Some days, I didn't tell her, I even felt good about it. But not when I felt like I did that day, and at that particular moment, as I opened the front door.

It wasn't just my injuries and thoughts of the receding cliff that made me feel like that. Someone had been inside my house again. You can always tell when you live alone. I could smell him, and it was a man. He wasn't a smoker either. No certain giveaway like that. But I still knew. It was . . . what? Someone else had been breathing the air in here. I could tell.

Nothing had been obviously moved but as I glanced around I could see one or two little signs. The keyboard for my desktop, for example. I keep it at a slight angle. That's what suits me. Now it was parallel to the desk edge. Someone had been at it again.

Doing what? There wasn't a lot on the computer for them to find. Perhaps they didn't need a lot? Just something in particular.

All I could think was that they had wanted

to check my emails, to see who or what I was sending out or receiving. Or to delete stuff, new stuff? That might explain the second visit.

To hell with it! I made for the kettle. 'Coffee?'

'That would be lovely, Frank. Thank you. But you sit down! I'll make it.'

I shook my head as gently as I could. 'I'm better on my feet for the moment. I was too long in the Land Rover.'

'Do you want to lie down?' she asked, sounding anxious.

'No. I'll be all right. I just need to straighten out some creases.'

While I waited for the kettle, I opened the computer up to check my emails. No important new ones. But one thing struck me instantly. The email I had received from Mike Rogers was gone, deleted.

I nodded with satisfaction. That was one thing my mystery intruder must have come for. Now there was no visible connection to PortPlus. So even if there had been some doubt in my mind, I was quite certain now they were dirty. It felt like progress.

Nancy was exploring, examining the view out of the kitchen window, picking up ornamental bits and pieces, studying my bookshelves.

I smiled, glad to have her company. 'I've got a bit more room for junk than you have in your place.'

She laughed. 'In my place,' she said, 'I have room for nothing at all. I can't even get all the useful stuff I need inside, never mind junk.'

That made me wonder where she kept her things. People who have emigrated usually have more than I'd seen in her hut. On the other hand, of course, people who have to leave a country in a hurry often have nothing at all with them.

'Did you have to get out fast?'

She turned and stared at me, knowing what I meant. Then she nodded. 'Very fast.'

It was an awkward moment. I felt I was in danger of trespassing where she didn't want me to go.

'Tell you what,' I said, changing the subject. 'Look upstairs, and sort out some bedding for the spare room. You'll find what you need in the cupboard on the landing. I'll give you a shout when the coffee's ready.'

'I'll do it afterwards,' she said. 'Let's have the coffee first.'

So we did. I made the coffee and we sat down with it at the kitchen table. Then I told her a little about life at Risky Point, until we were interrupted. A knock on the door and a shout warned of Jimmy Mack's arrival.

'Come on in, Jimmy!'

The door opened and the man himself entered. He stared at Nancy, surprised. 'I didn't know you had a visitor,' he said awkwardly.

'Jimmy Mack!' Nancy said, jumping to her feet. 'Fancy seeing you here!'

She rushed over to give him a hug. His face lit up with astonished smiles and wrinkles. 'Young Nancy?' he whispered back to her, shocked beyond belief.

I shook my head, astonished, though I knew I shouldn't have been by anything involving Jimmy Mack.

'Sit down, Jim,' I said. 'You're just in time for coffee.'

23

'I knew her grandpa,' Jimmy told me when things had settled down again, 'but I haven't seen her for many a year.'

'We still recognized each other, though,' Nancy contributed.

Jimmy grinned and shook his head, as if it was a mystery to him how these things worked. I knew exactly how he felt.

'You might have said,' I complained to Nancy.

She just shrugged and focussed all her attention on Jimmy. In turn, he was delighted to be the centre of attention. I couldn't blame him. It wasn't often he found himself in that position. For a time my aches and pains disappeared, overwhelmed by the joyous reunion being enacted before my very eyes.

All the same, I was puzzled, and even a little disconcerted, by the way Nancy had kept quiet about knowing Jimmy. It was on a par with how she had suddenly blurted out 'Mining' and 'Africa' to Henry. Hidden depths, or evasion? Anyway, I was glad she was here, and I looked forward to finding out what else she knew — and I didn't!

Now the initial adrenaline rush was over, Jimmy started peering at me closely and looking worried.

'You don't look well, son,' he said eventually. 'What's happened?'

'I ran into a bit of trouble, Jim.' I shrugged. 'Rather, it ran into me.'

'That's why I'm here,' Nancy said briskly. 'I came to look after him, and drive for him.'

Jimmy looked from one to the other of us. Amusement was irritatingly all over his face. So I told him briefly what had happened. Then I asked him if anything unusual had happened lately, or if he'd seen any strangers hanging around.

'I'm not sure,' he said, thinking about it. 'I've thought once or twice someone was around, up to no good. Just little things, you know. But I've not actually seen anyone.'

'What sort of things, Jim?'

He wiped his nose with the back of his hand thoughtfully. 'A flash of light, like someone was using field glasses. The feeling that someone was watching me. Then yesterday something startled a flock of finches out of that hawthorn over there. Not much, but . . .'

'Don't worry, Jim. They'll be watching me, not you, if anyone is around.'

I didn't want to worry him, not around his

own home. I didn't want him sitting on his front doorstep with a loaded shotgun either. So I didn't tell him someone had been through my house at least a couple of times. I just told him to let me know if he did see anyone.

He shook his head when I had finished. 'It all comes back to that MP, doesn't it?' he said wonderingly. 'If you'd never gone to the Gare that afternoon . . . '

'Don't go there, Jim!' I said with a groan. 'I've done enough wishful thinking for myself.'

He grinned and looked at Nancy.

'We've been looking into this company that's threatening the fishermen's huts at the South Gare,' she said. 'And the seals and fishermen, and everything else. And guess what?'

Jimmy waited expectantly.

'It doesn't appear to exist,' Nancy said triumphantly. 'So we really do have a mystery to solve. We started off trying to find James Campbell's killers. Now we don't know where it's going to lead.'

Nancy taking over! I thought ruefully. I guessed I might have to get used to that if I retained her services as a driver.

Jimmy looked at me, eyebrows raised in enquiry.

I shrugged. 'Someone has to find out what happened.'

'And it has to be you? Not Bill Peart?'

'Well . . . Tell you what, Jim. If someone pokes you in the eye, are you just going to let them get away with it?'

He began to laugh then. It wasn't long before all three of us were laughing. It was a mad situation.

★　★　★

After Jimmy had gone, I moved on to the sofa and let Nancy have a bath and sort out the bedding for the spare room. I was glad to be left alone for a while. I needed a bit of thinking space.

Dead as he was, James Campbell was still at the top of my agenda. The key to everything that had been happening to me was James Campbell himself. Something he had been doing, or that he represented, had triggered all this mayhem and duplicity. Could it really just be his opposition to PortPlus's plans? When the company didn't appear to exist!

I couldn't unlock the puzzle myself. Not yet. Maybe Henry would, as he looked up Donovan McCardle. Mining and Africa. That's what Nancy had suggested he focus on. Interesting. I wondered why she had said that. Obviously, she knew more than she had told me so far.

* * *

Nancy returned and announced herself satisfied with her room. 'Such a wonderful view!'

I smiled and nodded. 'Glad you like it.'

'And the bath was good, too. It's just a pity I didn't have any clean clothes to put on afterwards,' she added ruefully.

'You don't need to worry about that around here,' I told her. 'Jimmy Mack hasn't put clean clothes on since last year.'

She laughed. 'He's a grand old chap, isn't he?'

I nodded. 'A good friend and neighbour. Have a root around, by the way. If there's anything of mine that fits, you're welcome to try it on.'

'I was thinking underwear.'

'Ah! That might be a problem.'

Smiling, she looked at me and said, 'So what now? What are you thinking?'

'I was just thinking about James Campbell. I know next to nothing about him, but you seem to have known him quite well?'

She shrugged. 'I'm not sure about that. I'm

not sure anyone knew James well.'

'When we first met, you said that he had been helping with a problem the fishermen were having. The future of the huts, presumably?'

'That's right. I went to see him. We were all very worried about the rumours flying around.'

'Was there more to it than that?'

'We weren't in a relationship, if that's what you mean. We just became friends.' She shrugged and added, 'James was far too busy to have a relationship with anyone outside politics. His job, his work, was his life.'

That sounded right to me, from what I had learned of the man. He was a full-time Member of Parliament who seemed to work his socks off.

'How much time did he spend in his constituency?' I asked.

'He was here most weekends. During the week he was in London. That's pretty normal, I think.'

'So he lived here? I mean, he had a home to come back to?'

She chuckled. 'A home? I don't think so. You couldn't really say that. James lived out of his suitcase.'

'A place to stay, then. He had to have a place in the constituency, surely? If he came back every . . . '

'Oh, yes. He had a little house here. Pretty basic, but adequate.'

'You've been there?'

She nodded. 'Of course.'

Of course, I thought ironically. Of course she had. She'd been everywhere and knew everything.

'Right, then. That's what we'll do next,' I announced. 'Tomorrow morning we'll go and have a look at James' house. OK?'

'OK,' she said with a shrug.

Getting information out of her was like pulling teeth, but at least I'd done it. I had found out something else I hadn't known. That was enough for one day.

★ ★ ★

Campbell's house was on the edge of Ormesby, once a quiet, historic village, now little more than a distant suburb of Middlesbrough. Green fields were still close, though. Nancy parked on the cobbles outside the house and we sat for a few moments while I sized it up.

Built of local sandstone, with Welsh slate for the roof. Bow windows. Entered direct from the street, no doubt with a garden at the back. A couple of hundred years old, and not mucked about. Simple, but attractive and no doubt pricey. A good investment.

'Nice,' I said. 'A little old country cottage.'
Nancy nodded.

'He didn't fancy living in the industrial heartland of his constituency?'

She shook her head. 'That's where all the problems are, and I never blamed him for wanting to have a break from them.'

I could understand that. In a way, I had wanted much the same for myself.

'I wouldn't mind a look inside,' I said wistfully.

I still didn't have much of a feel for what the man had been like. Listening to what other people thought didn't tell me everything.

'We can go inside if you want to,' Nancy said.

'Better not. Breaking into a murdered person's home doesn't go down very well with the law.'

'I'm not talking about breaking in,' she said patiently.

I just looked at her.

'I know where there's a key.'

I didn't bother asking how or why she knew.

'Let's go, then,' I said.

★   ★   ★

Campbell had kept a bunch of spare keys under a flowerpot in the back garden. Nancy knew that. I was no longer surprised by the things she knew and said, and could do; I accepted her knowledge and capabilities as I would have accepted any other windfall.

The cottage was small. It had a couple of rooms plus a kitchen downstairs, and two bedrooms and a bathroom upstairs. The furnishings were basic, adequate, no more. They were all a man needed in a weekend retreat.

In fact, the best thing about it for me was the three pictures of Old Middlesbrough hanging on the north-facing wall in the main living room. They were stunning, two of them big as well as colourful. The big ones were awash with dreamy light, as coal poured from staithes into waiting colliers, and men sweated and worked in the light from the flames of a blast furnace. The third picture was different, and done by a different hand. Detailed, meticulous and equally atmospheric, it showed a late-Victorian evening scene of rain-wet streets shining beneath gas lamps near the Royal Exchange building.

I moved on and checked the bookcase. Nothing special there: a collection of political memoirs and recent history. A framed photograph held an image of a younger James

Campbell and two older people who I took to be his parents. Nancy confirmed it.

The dining room contained table and chairs, and not much else. Upstairs, there were a few clothes in a wardrobe and in a chest of drawers in one of the bedrooms. They included a business suit and some casual, weekend-type stuff. Campbell hadn't been a fancy dresser.

I stood with my back to the bedroom window and glanced round. I didn't think I had missed anything.

'He didn't spend a lot of time here,' Nancy said, as if divining my surprise at how little there was in the house, and how basic it was.

I nodded. 'Too busy, I suppose.'

'He was just here for weekends, and by the time he'd done his surgeries and met his agent to discuss constituency affairs — not to mention attending a couple of fundraisers — it was time to get back to London. He didn't even have time to read the Sunday papers until he got back on the train.'

I gave her a wry smile.

'I suppose,' she qualified.

'You don't have to pretend with me, Nancy,' I said with a chuckle. 'I realize you must have known James a lot better than you've been letting on.'

She coloured and looked indignant for a

moment. 'It's not true!' she said. 'Well, only partly.'

I nodded and started for the stairs.

'James was gay,' she said after me. 'We simply weren't interested in each other in the way you obviously mean.'

I stopped and turned back to her.

'We were just friends,' she said flatly.

'Oh?' I nodded then. 'I understand.'

'Do you really?'

'I think so. I'm sorry I misjudged the situation. Let's go back downstairs. You can tell me about those pictures.'

'Oh, them!' she said with a sigh. 'Terrible, aren't they?'

Well, they were too much, perhaps, for the living room wall of a simple country cottage, but I certainly wouldn't have called them terrible. Not at all. If nothing else, they were interesting scenes from a Middlesbrough that no longer existed.

The two big ones were romantic essays in industrial history. Very Turner-ish. Billowing clouds, the sun breaking through the half-light while men went about their hard labour. The romance of industry, as eminent Victorians used to say.

'Family heirlooms,' Nancy said dismissively, with a yawn.

'Really?'

Staring at them, I wondered if they were originals.

'James told me they had been in the family home in Africa for years and years. As a boy, he stared at them so much there was only one place he wanted to come to when he left Africa. He just had to see the place that had inspired the pictures.'

'And he brought them with him?'

She nodded.

'How had they got out to Africa in the first place?'

'Some relative had emigrated from here, and taken them with him or bought them later. I'm not sure exactly.'

'Presumably the relative got sick of looking at lions and giraffes, and things?'

Nancy smiled. 'I'm sure you're right. Now, I suppose, I'll get them.'

'Oh?'

'James said I could have them. He'd got bored with them.'

'They'll look good in your hut.'

She laughed. 'I'll have to build an extension for them!'

She would indeed. A gallery even! I shook my head and smiled at the thought.

'Come on, then. Let's get going.'

I took a last look at the paintings. They were impressive. More than that, I liked them, all three of them. If they did pass down to Nancy, and if she really didn't like them, I might offer her a few quid for them. I had plenty of bare walls needing adornment.

I followed Nancy back outside, and let her lock up and return the keys to their resting place. It looked to me as if she had done that often enough before, and I wondered if she had told the truth about her relationship with James Campbell.

Mystery girl! I'd been lucky to find her. Or was it she who had found me?

24

Nancy wanted to get back to the South Gare, and her boat and hut, and I was feeling much better. So I dropped her off there and headed home, having agreed to keep her informed of progress, if any. Nothing much had happened between us but I think we knew by then that we would see each other again very soon, progress or not. The vibes between us said so.

I appreciated the help Nancy had given me. But I needed to sort my head out and get things straight. I needed to stand back from her, as well, and think about things she had said — and not said. There were some pretty big questions still to be answered, much as I liked her. Such as how well had she really known James Campbell — and was he really gay? Also: what did she know about Donovan McCardle — and mining in Africa?

There were still plenty of questions that had nothing to do with Nancy, of course. Who were the three guys who had kicked my ribs in, for instance? And who were they working for? PortPlus — even though it didn't seem to exist? McCardle?

So I was all set to get home and give it a

rest. Talk to Jimmy Mack about other things, or have a lie on the bed while my bones did some more knitting together. Then I thought to hell with it, and turned round and ran back to Middlesbrough to see Henry.

★ ★ ★

'Come on in, Frank.'

I shut the door behind me.

'Am I glad to see you,' he said.

'Why? Do you want some money off me?'

'Not yet.' He peered at his computer screen a moment longer and then turned round to engage with me.

'How are you getting on?' I asked him.

'That McCardle feller is, or was, big in mining in Africa — very big.'

'Was he? So Nancy gave us a good clue.'

He nodded. '*Was* is the operative word, though. He's not big now. He's got nowt now, in fact.'

'Go on.'

'Chrome mining. That's what it was. A big chrome mine. But Mugabe took it off him. Returned it to the people, I should say.'

'So McCardle was in Zimbabwe?'

'Mostly.'

Henry shrugged and added, 'I almost feel sorry for him. He was chairman of the company that had developed a major mine there. Very valuable it was, too. But it was taken over by the Government and he was kicked out.

'Some of Mugabe's cronies have it now, not that they'll know what to do with it. It will probably return to bush, like a lot of farms and industry in Zimbabwe.'

I thought about the implications. One very obvious one was that if McCardle was skint, he had had to find a new way of making a living. So he'd come to England. But how could someone in his position plan to take over Teesport? How could he assemble the money?

I had no idea. I know plenty about small business, but the mega corporations and global investment funds are way out of my league. And they were what was involved here.

'He has a sidekick,' Henry added. 'A Mike Rogers. Do you know him, as well?'

'Yes.' I nodded. 'The Chief Executive. I know the pair of them. The famous PortPlus duo.'

'Well, the two of them exist,' Henry said with satisfaction, 'if nothing else does. But they have no money.'

* * *

I left Henry's place having convinced myself it was all a con trick. I didn't know how it would work, but that was what it was. No way in the world could you take PortPlus seriously now. In a way, it was a relief. There was nothing for anyone to worry about. It was just fluff. Smoke and mirrors. We could all get on with our lives and forget about the whole damned thing. Nancy was going to be pleased to hear it, and she wouldn't be the only one.

There remained the murder of James Campbell, of course. That hadn't gone away.

As I was passing the railway station a newspaper hoarding caught my eye. I stopped and looked at it. Then I bought a copy of the evening paper.

I waited till I was in a coffee shop before I unfolded the paper and looked at the front page. Then I collected my Americano and shuffled off to a quiet corner with it. I sat down, poured milk into the coffee, glowered at a ridiculous modern artwork on the wall, and finally smoothed out the paper on the tabletop to read.

I'd been wrong again. PortPlus were still a player.

It was all there, on the front page of the *Evening Gazette*. The offer to shareholders, and the terse advice from Teesport to their shareholders to reject the offer. So it was genuine, after all. A hostile takeover bid had been launched. The wraps were off. A smiling McCardle was out in the open now, along with Mike Rogers. The pair of them photographed standing on the front steps of their new corporate home, a castle in the Cleveland Hills.

Also on the front page was a summary of all the good things PortPlus would bring to the area. The riverside would be tidied up. New industrial areas would be created, along with a new nuclear power station on the south side, not far from the steelworks. Executive houses with their own riverside access and marina would be created. No end of stuff. Most of all, of course, there would be new jobs, jobs by the tens of thousands.

It was too much. I was stunned. I jammed the folded paper in my pocket and got up to leave the café. Could they really pull it off? I didn't know now.

I could see the attraction of what was proposed. Who couldn't? But was the proposal real, or just a flight of fantasy? There had to be something solid there. There just had to be. Otherwise, what was in it for McCardle?

These were big questions, too big for me. I clung to the thought that the main actors were dirty, and played very dirty. It was more than likely that they had commissioned the murder of James Campbell when he had got in their way, and now I was in their way. It was a worrying thought.

Something had to be done about them. I was in no doubt about that. Somehow they had to be exposed. Unfortunately, I couldn't see anyone else but me — and Henry and Nancy — trying to do anything about that.

25

Back at Risky Point, I did ordinary things for a while as I tried to settle down and work out a sensible approach to the problems confronting me. There were things to do in the house, the routine, domestic things that are easy to neglect when you're solving murders and world problems — not to mention talking to the likes of Bill Peart and Jimmy Mack, and chasing around with strange women like Nancy Peters.

I'm the kind of single fellow who likes to live in a clean house and sleep between laundered sheets. When it comes to food and cooking I go for the easy stuff that I can get together quickly, but I do wear clean clothes and ironed shirts. I probably wouldn't get much business if I didn't. Not every potential client is looking for a beach bum.

So I did some catching up that evening, and then had a good night's sleep. I was feeling optimistic, and my injuries were mending. I would have liked to invite Nancy back to Risky Point, but as far as I knew she had no vehicle. Coming here by boat was not something I could ever have recommended.

So I would wait to see her again.

The next morning, I took advantage of low tide to walk on the beach. It was a raw sort of day, with threatening dark cloud and a cold wind off the sea, but it was good to be out. I felt better in the open air. I even did some stretches and jogged a short distance. I was on recovery road.

The climb back up the track had me breathing hard and thinking of a hot shower before I went to meet Nancy again. A man seemed to be waiting for me near the top of the track. He watched me labour up the slope, waiting patiently.

'Good morning!' he called as I drew near. 'Mr Doy?'

'Yes. How can I help you?'

I was only ten yards from him by then. I wondered what he wanted. It was unusual to meet anyone here. He knew my name. So he hadn't lost his way, which was the first thought that had come to mind.

'I needed to make sure,' he replied.

I tripped and stumbled slightly. As I straightened up, my eyes met his and I realized instantly this was not a friendly encounter.

Then I caught a glimpse of a hand dipping beneath his jacket. As it emerged again, I could see the hand was not empty.

There wasn't time to register the make of

gun. Instinctively, I hurled myself forward and dived at his legs. He was still upslope from me and I reached out and swung an arm, catching him behind the knees. His legs buckled and he lurched back to avoid falling forwards.

I hit the ground hard and pain screamed through my damaged ribs. Ignoring it, I bounced up and threw myself forward desperately. Somehow I caught him before he'd recovered his balance and knocked him backwards again. It was my chance. I went with him, clawing at the hand holding the gun.

He wasn't big. More lean and wiry. But he was strong. I was heavier than him, though, and sensed that I had an edge at close quarters. But, God, he was strong!

He fought like a fury. We both did. He kneed me in the groin, hurting but not paralyzing. I smashed an elbow into his face and blood spurted from his broken nose. I hung onto the hand holding the gun with both of my hands and ground it against the rock, enduring the blows to my head that came from his free hand.

The punching stopped. The fingers locked onto the gun weakened. I tore the gun out of his hand, but failed to hold onto it. The gun fell out of reach.

Sensing a diversionary tactic I turned quickly.

His free hand now held a knife. He jabbed it at my belly. I parried the movement with my forearm and turned him, pushing him away.

It was a mistake. I had given him space to swing at me. I pulled back frantically and kicked out, trying to win distance from the knife.

He came forward, weaving, the knife flashing. I was higher than him now and managed to kick out and stamp him in the chest. He grunted and stumbled backwards, struggling to keep his balance.

I slipped myself and fell flat on my back, but scrambled round onto my knees, ready for the next charge.

It didn't come.

He wasn't there.

Bewildered, I jumped up, desperate to avoid his knife. Then I realized he really wasn't there.

He had gone over the cliff edge. The knife had gone, too. And the gun.

I was alone, and all I could hear was the sound of my own hoarse breathing.

I could scarcely believe it. I got up and peered over the edge of the path, down to the sea. Nothing. I stared hard, but I could see no sign of him in the white water crashing onto huge boulders.

The water was deep immediately below where I was standing. He would have hit one of the many big rocks protruding from the sea before disappearing into it. Even if he had somehow missed the rocks, the sea would still have claimed him. I was sure of that. He couldn't have survived.

I sat back and held my hands to my face for a moment, waiting for the pain the struggle had re-energized to pass. I wondered who he was, who he had been. A man. That was all I knew. A man who had been intent on killing me.

★　★　★

Bill Peart was at his most sensitive when he turned up a bit later. The uniforms had arrived first once again but there hadn't been much for them to do. They just guarded the crime scene until Bill arrived and told them to check down on the beach.

'What happened this time?' he asked when we were alone.

'This time?'

I stared hard at him until he shook his head and sighed. 'Were you just in the wrong place again?'

'It was more than that, Bill. The guy was here to kill me. First he needed to be sure he'd got the right man. He called my name to make certain. But it still didn't work out for him. That's all I can tell you.'

'And in the struggle he went over the edge of the cliff?'

'I got lucky,' I admitted, nodding. 'It was very nearly me that took the drop.'

We trudged back to the house, went inside and sat down. Bill sat up straight, on duty. 'Who was he?' he asked.

I shook my head. 'I've never seen him before. From his accent, in the few words he spoke, I would guess he was American. Otherwise, all I know is he was a tough little bugger.'

'Any idea why you were targeted?'

'Yes, I have,' I said ruefully. 'It's not the first time I've been attacked.'

I told him again about the beating I'd been given by the Geordies. Then I told him someone had been going through my house and checking my computer files.

'It all seems to be to do with me having been at the South Gare that day when Campbell was killed,' I concluded.

He nodded.

'I think PortPlus are behind it. They were trying to make me keep out of it by issuing warnings and making the job offer. That failed. So they decided to go for the next best thing, and get rid of me altogether.'

My story made him uneasy. I could see

why. There was no direct evidence for my suspicions and allegations. On the other hand, I was his friend. He knew that, for whatever reason, I really had been in danger, and probably was still.

'The Geordies who beat you up and the guy who came here to kill you are different animals,' he pointed out. 'What does that tell you?'

'It tells me they ran out of patience.'

'Maybe. And someone's been in your house without kicking the door in. That doesn't sound like the Geordie gang.'

'More like the man waiting on the path for me?' I suggested.

'Could be two different lots, working for two different clients.'

PortPlus and someone else? It was possible, I supposed. But it seemed unlikely.

'You need protection,' Bill said, snapping out of it.

I shook my head. 'We've been through that before. I'm staying here, and I don't want anyone with me.'

'Unless it's a woman?'

I grinned. 'Women in uniform don't attract me. So you can forget that!'

He got up to go. Some things, he knew, he just couldn't do anything about.

'Call me,' he said, 'when the next surprise happens to you.'

26

I took out the newspaper with all the good news about the official launch of PortPlus and read through the main story again, in case I had missed something. I hadn't. Pushing the paper away, I considered what to do next.

I needed to talk to Nancy, to bring her up to speed. She could be at risk herself now, because of her association with me. What to do about that was an open question. I would have to see how she took the news. First, though, I had to get there and talk to her.

Before I left, I dug out a spare mobile to give her. From now on, I wanted to be able to speak to her without having to drive to the South Gare to do it.

The road through what was left of ruined Warrenby, a former industrial village adjoining Redcar, was busy. A stream of vehicles was pouring out of the steelworks as a shift ended. It was small beer compared with how the whole of Teesside used to be when shifts in the works ended, but at least it was evidence of a thousand jobs saved.

Past the works, the road to the South Gare

narrowed to a single lane bordered by sand dunes covered with marram grass. On the broader, seaward side, there were still a few wartime relics remaining in the dunes: pill boxes and concrete gun emplacements half-buried in the sand. On the river side, there wasn't much space at all before the drop down to the river at high tide, and an expanse of sand at low tide.

Gulls swept by overhead, endlessly searching. Oyster-catchers hunted down on the wet sand. The marram grass bent and rustled in the stiff breeze. The Gare drew close. In a short distance I had entered another world. I parked near the huts and went looking for Nancy.

She wasn't at home. I looked around the immediate vicinity but didn't find her. It was very quiet. One or two cars, but hardly anyone in sight. Happily, the two old codgers I had spoken to before were there again, sitting around the stove, the door to their hut wide open.

'If you didn't put so much wood in the stove,' I told them, 'it wouldn't get so hot. Then you wouldn't have to have the door open all the time.'

'Is that right?' Glasses said. 'But then we wouldn't see clever buggers like you poking about where you're not wanted, would we?'

I laughed.

'What did he say, Willy?' the deaf one asked.

'He's complaining about the heat from the stove, Jack.'

'Is he now?' Jack glowered at me and said, 'Wait till you're our age! You need a bit of heat at our time of life.'

I nodded and said I could understand that. Then I asked Willy if he'd seen Nancy.

'You're not the first to ask me that today,' he said suspiciously.

'Oh?'

'There was three blokes here a while ago looking for her.'

My head jerked and my heart began to beat faster. I didn't like the sound of that.

'Three? Did they say who they were?'

He shook his head. 'Never seen them before either. We didn't like the look of 'em, to tell you the truth.'

I was pretty sure who they were. I just hoped I wasn't too late.

'Who are you anyway?' he added. 'We'd never seen you either till the other day.'

'Frank Doy.'

'Never heard of you.'

'What did he say?' Jack asked, leaning forward to catch what he could.

'He says his name's Frank Doy,' Willy

replied in a voice that could probably have been heard several miles away in Redcar.

Jack shook his head. He hadn't heard of me either.

'She won't have gone out in her boat?' I asked.

'Nancy?' Willy shook his head doubtfully. 'I couldn't tell you. Like I told them others, I have no idea where she is.'

We weren't getting anywhere fast. I chewed at a ragged edge on my thumbnail. Then inspiration struck.

'I'm a neighbour, and a friend, of Jimmy Mack's,' I said quietly, confidentially.

There was a moment of silence. Willy studied me astutely and then said, 'From Skinningrove?'

I shook my head. 'Risky Point. That's where we live. The old cottages.'

He positively beamed now. 'You should have said!'

'What's that?' Jack demanded.

'He's a neighbour of Jimmy Mack's!'

Recognition dawned there, too. A big smile broke out.

'How is he?' Willy demanded.

'Good. He's good.'

They gave me their names then, and I promised to tell Jimmy to pay them a visit soon.

'So what's all this about the men looking for Nancy?' I asked when it was possible to get back to business.

'I didn't like the look of them,' Willy said again. 'Tough bunch, and not from round here.'

'Geordies, were they?'

He nodded. 'They could have been. I told them nowt.'

'What about Nancy?'

'I haven't seen her this morning.'

There were plenty of places she could be. She might even have walked along the beach to Redcar.

'And she won't be out with the boat?'

'She could be, but she'll not be fishing if she is. The tide's wrong.'

All the same, I thought, she might have taken it out to get away from people she didn't want to find her.

'What's it called, her boat?'

Willy chuckled. '*Nancy Baby*! That's her grandad for you, calling it that.'

I smiled and thanked them. Then I made my way over to Paddy's Hole, not sure I wanted to find the boat still there. If it was, it might mean she'd been found by the Geordies. If it wasn't there, how the hell was I going to find her anyway? I was seriously worried.

Nancy Baby was there. It was a typical small coble, one of a dozen or more in Paddy's Hole. Its main distinguishing feature was that it was sunk, with just a couple of feet at the front end sticking out of the water. When the tide came in, there wouldn't even be that much to see. Someone — I could guess who — had hammered a gaping hole low down in the side.

So Nancy hadn't got away in the boat. Someone had made sure of that. I didn't despair. It could mean she was still around, and they were still looking for her. I decided to cling to that hope.

But where could she be? I spun round and considered the huts and boats around Paddy's Hole. No end of possible hiding places. Then there were all the other little mooring places and jetties, and all the abandoned, derelict sheds and old brick buildings. Not to mention the fifty-odd huts around her own place. Always assuming she hadn't simply walked away — or been found.

I was very worried for her. The three men looking for her were the ones who I believed had killed James Campbell. And they were close.

I walked around, showing myself in the

open. If Nancy was in hiding, she might see me and come out. The men looking for her might see me as well, of course. If that happened, I would be on the phone to Bill Peart without any hesitation.

I walked to the end of the breakwater and back, without seeing Nancy or anyone else. On the return leg, I scanned the dunes stretching away towards Redcar, and wondered if there might be a hunt going on somewhere in there. Impossible to say. There was no point going to look either. I might come across people I didn't want to meet. Better to stay somewhere more public.

But there were limits to my patience. Eventually I decided there were better things to do than hang around indefinitely, waiting. I checked Nancy's hut once more. Then I headed back to the Land Rover.

★ ★ ★

That's where she was. She was sitting in the front passenger seat, waiting for me.

'What kept you?' she demanded.

I chuckled, gave her a hug of relief and got in and started the engine.

'Where are we going?' she asked.

'Back to Risky Point,' I told her. 'I feel safer there.'

'Me, too,' she said.

'You know three men are looking for you?'

'I saw them.'

'They're the same ones who threw James off the end of the breakwater and knocked me about.'

'I guessed.'

'Where are they now?'

She shrugged. 'Gone, I think.'

'Thank God for that! I'm sorry about your boat, by the way. Did they do that?'

She nodded and grimaced. 'Bastards!'

'We'll get it fixed.'

'You think? Is that possible?'

'Of course it is. I know people who can take care of that very easily. Don't worry.'

She smiled and kissed me on the cheek. 'You're a wonderful man,' she said.

That made me actually feel rather wonderful. So we set off happily on the long, thin road away from the South Gare.

We got half a mile or so. Then, just where the road does a little kink through the dunes, we found a big pickup straddling the road, blocking our way. I recognized the two men standing beside it. The third was in the cab.

'It's them!' Nancy gasped.

She was right. And there wasn't much I could do about it.

27

There really wasn't much choice. Instinct and reflexes took over, and I did what came naturally. I shifted down a gear and jammed my foot on the accelerator.

The engine screamed and the steering wheel juddered. I yelled at Nancy to brace herself. Then I wrenched the steering wheel round, aimed at the back end of the truck and gritted my teeth.

Jimmy Mack had recently helped me fit a winch I'd picked up at a scrap yard on to the front of the Land Rover. We'd thought it might come in handy for hauling his boat out of the water. I had a very different use for it in mind now.

We hit the truck at the back end of the load deck and I was flung forward until the seat belt stopped me. The projecting winch dug hard into the truck and my nerves went mad as my ears filled with the screeching of tortured metal.

I held on and kept my foot on the throttle. Coming in at an angle, we were still moving and turning the truck, but not fast enough. Momentum had gone with the impact. We needed to get out.

I wrenched the wheel round and the winch came away from the body of the truck. A gap appeared between us and the nearest sand dune. I made for it. Our offside wheels dropped off the tarmac and began to spin in soft sand. I eased back on the throttle but managed to keep us going until we were through the gap and could get all four wheels back onto pavement again. Then we were off!

There was damage. I could hear something banging and rattling at the front end. Somehow the windscreen had cracked and splintered, and I could see that Nancy's window had disappeared. But it was no time to be stopping for an audit.

'You all right?' I shouted over the roar of the engine.

I glanced sideways and she nodded. She was tight-lipped and covered in shards of glass from the broken window.

'Hang on!' I called. 'We'll stop somewhere soon.'

Somewhere safe, I meant. We couldn't stop here.

But the truck was not following. In the rear-view mirror I saw men milling around it. The front end was buried in soft sand. We had won ourselves some time.

I kept going hard until we reached

Warrenby a few minutes later. Then I eased off. Soon afterwards I turned off the main road and into the old Coatham High Street. Then I stopped, keeping the engine running, and hauled out my phone.

'Frank?' Nancy said quietly.

'I'm calling up the cavalry.'

Bill Peart must have been at his desk. He answered the phone immediately.

'What do you want this time, Frank?'

It was always the same. If he wanted me, any time would do. If I wanted him, it was always an inconvenience.

'The three guys I saw after James Campbell was put in the water? I've just had a run-in with them on the road past Tod Point to the South Gare. Their truck is stuck in soft sand. If you're quick . . . '

'Right. Got that.'

He broke the connection.

I shook my head, impressed. He could be a ball of fire when it suited him.

Nancy had got out of the cab to dust broken glass off herself. I motioned to her to climb back inside. I wanted to get moving again.

'Who did you call?' she demanded to know as we picked up speed.

'The cops. There's just a chance they might be able to pick them up.'

184

'Who did you call?' she insisted.

'A pal. Bill Peart, a detective inspector.'

'Must be nice to have connections like that.'

'Not always, it isn't. But on occasion . . . '

I left it there. I didn't think Bill would be able to move fast enough to grab them, but there was a chance.

'You all right?' I asked again.

She nodded. 'Just a bit shaken up. That's all.'

She paused and then added, 'Someone fired a gun at us, Frank.'

I grimaced. No wonder the glass had broken!

'All I can say, Nancy, is that if I'd stopped, it could have been a lot worse.'

'I know.' She shook her head and added, 'They mean it, those people, don't they?'

She was right. They were playing for keeps. Us or them.

'They're the ones who dumped James off the breakwater,' I told her. 'And I'm the witness they want to eliminate. Unfortunately, they've linked you with me now.'

'That's not why they were after me,' she said.

'It is,' I assured her. 'But let's not argue about it.'

She didn't reply.

I set course for Risky Point. Perhaps I was kidding myself, but I felt we would be safer on my home ground.

*   *   *

We were both quiet the rest of the way. Nancy was subdued and very obviously upset. I began to wonder if I was right in assuming the Geordies had gone after her because of her association with me. Would they have known about that yet?

And what had she meant when she disagreed with me about why they were after her? An alternative explanation was that they had targeted her because she had been close to James Campbell and was herself a critic of PortPlus, although she certainly wasn't alone in that respect. Surely they couldn't be planning to murder all their critics?

*   *   *

Back at Risky Point, I let Nancy into the house.

'What are you going to do?' she asked as I turned away.

'I want to check the Land Rover over. See what the damage is.'

'It needs new windows,' she said with a

186

rueful grin, beginning to recover.

'I hope that's all it needs.'

I couldn't find much wrong that I didn't already know about. The winch at the front end had taken the hit, and had served us well. It was a bit twisted and out of position, but the back-end of the Geordies' truck must have looked a lot worse. The winch was a big lump of heavy metal. It would have torn a lump out of their vehicle.

What I really needed to do, though, was get the Land Rover up on a ramp and check underneath. It was possible that the frame had been twisted and knocked out of true. But I hadn't time to do that myself.

I phoned a guy I knew with a garage in Skelton.

'What have you done?' he shouted over the noise in the workshop. 'Rolled it?'

I winced. 'Now, now, Eric! I'm not that bad a driver. But I did have a bit of a bump. Can you take it in and check it over? Fix the glass — and anything else that needs doing?'

'Can it be driven?'

'Well . . . Not comfortably. Maybe not safely either.'

'I'll bring Jessie over, then,' he shouted again as the decibel count at his end rose to a horrendous level. 'You'll be wanting wheels, I take it?'

'I'd be stuck without them.'

'The lad can bring you something.'

'Nothing fancy, mind! I don't want something that will turn heads when I go past.'

Eric chuckled. 'What you want is a stealth vehicle, right? Something that will slip under the radar?'

'Exactly.'

'I'll see what we've got.'

I switched off and turned to see that Nancy had appeared with a couple of mugs of coffee.

'Who's Jessie?' she asked.

'You heard him, did you?'

'I couldn't avoid hearing him.'

I grinned. 'Jessie is Eric's recovery vehicle. He named her after his mother.'

'Nice.'

I sipped the coffee, my eyes still on the Land Rover, and added, 'It's going into the garage. I'm getting Eric to fix things. I haven't time myself.'

'You wouldn't consider writing it off, and getting a new one?'

I shook my head. 'Not after all the hours I've put in restoring it.'

'That's what I like about you,' she said with a smile. 'You don't do things the easy way.'

Even though I laughed, I knew she wasn't far wrong.

'When we've finished the coffee,' I suggested, 'how about a walk on the beach? Blow the cobwebs away?'

'I'd like that,' she said. 'I would like it very much.'

There was a look in her eye I hadn't seen before. It made me feel good, better anyway.

*   *   *

We made our way down the rough track to the little beach at the base of the cliffs. It was a journey I had made countless times, and the exposure didn't bother me, but Nancy struggled to conceal her apprehension. She hung on to me gratefully when I offered a helping hand. I didn't tell her about my recent struggle there.

'It used to be a six-lane highway,' I told her, 'but one day the sea took most of it away.'

She had the grace to chuckle. 'One day?'

'Well, over time.'

'It's far too dangerous. They should put up a no-entry sign.'

'It's all right when it's dry. It's just in the wet it can be a bit difficult.'

The conversation had got us past the place where I had had the fight, without her noticing anything. I hoped we wouldn't find a body at the bottom of the path.

'You're lucky the sea didn't take your cottage, as well as the path,' Nancy said.

'It will one day, but not for a while yet, I hope. Anyway, Jimmy Mack's place is closer to the edge than mine and he says he's not moving. So I can't either.'

She laughed and clung to me harder. Suddenly, not really surprising ourselves, we were kissing. The moment had been a while coming, but I don't believe either of us had doubted that it would.

'Will it really happen, do you think?' she asked when we broke apart and continued on our way.

'The cottage collapsing? One day it will. I just hope it won't be in my time.'

I hugged her hard to persuade her I wasn't worried. She laughed again, and I felt her relax. The distraction had helped overcome her apprehension. We made it to the bottom without any further difficulty.

'It's wonderful here,' she whispered, turning round to give the little beach and the big sea all her attention. 'Absolutely gorgeous!'

'I like it,' I admitted.

I liked her, as well. I liked that she had recovered so fast from her ordeal that day. Most of all, though, I liked the feel and the scent of her, and the way she had of saying surprising things. I was very glad she was here with me.

She took my hand and held it. I put an arm around her, and gently squeezed. She raised her face and I kissed her again. We parted with a smile, knowing that even better things were to come. Then we turned to walk the couple of hundred yards that was as far as we could go before the cliff stuck out into deep water.

'Is that Jimmy Mack's boat?' she asked, looking at the coble pulled up high against the foot of the cliff.

'It is. And they're his huts.'

There were three of them. One had always been his. The others had become his when their original owners faded away.

We spent half an hour down there, listening to the sea and the gulls, and watching distant ships. It was a good, peaceful time. The turmoil of the day settled.

'Let's go back,' Nancy said suddenly.

She was right. It was time. We both knew that. It was how things were between us.

28

I had just taken the top off a boiled egg when I heard a growling noise outside. It was coming closer. Nancy looked at me anxiously.

I waited until the familiar yellow and blue zig-zags came into view through the kitchen window. Then I pronounced.

'It's my pal, Bill Peart.'

'The cop?'

I nodded. 'A pal, and a cop.'

She screwed up her face with displeasure.

'He's a good guy,' I said gently.

She laughed, said she was sure he was and announced that she was off to put some clothes on. It was disappointing. The view over the breakfast table until then had been exceptional, spectacular even.

I got up and opened the door. 'Morning, Bill!'

He looked at me suspiciously. 'What's got into you?' he demanded as he walked through the gate.

'Ever the sceptic and the cynic!'

'What's this?' he demanded, coming to a stop and surveying the table.

'Breakfast, Bill. Just breakfast. Want some? Toast, or an egg perhaps?'

'Just coffee.'

I could see his eyes had fastened on the second place setting, and the unfinished bowl of muesli.

'Jac here?'

'Not any more,' I said quietly, and with a wince, hoping he would get the message from the expression on my face.

'Not any more.' He repeated the phrase and followed up with a heavy sigh. 'What did I tell you?'

'I can't remember it all, Bill, to be honest. Was it something about getting a proper job? Meeting a better class of people?'

He took the mug of coffee I handed him and occupied a spare chair.

'Nancy will be down in a minute,' I told him gravely. 'She was with me at the Gare.'

'Nancy.' He nodded, kept a straight face and said, 'I'll try to remember that.'

'I'm not married, remember?' I pointed out.

'Indeed you're not, and you're not likely to be.' He sipped his coffee and added, 'And you don't work for my chief either.'

Whatever that had to do with it.

'Has he been giving you a hard time again?'

'Nothing out of the ordinary. He just wants this case cleared up fast, so he can get on with his golf without having to deal with a lot of questions from the media every five minutes.'

'Tell him it will take as long as it takes.'

'Thanks, Frank. I'll tell him that.'

His face brightened as feet clattered on the stairs and Nancy came into view.

'Good morning, Nancy!' he boomed.

She gave him an uncertain smile and glanced at me.

'Don't mind Bill,' I told her wearily. 'He thinks he's a comedian.'

'Good morning, Mr Bill!' she said brightly then.

He laughed. 'Come on,' he said. 'Finish your breakfast. I just stopped by to tell Frank the latest.'

'Did you catch them?' I asked.

He shook his head. 'Just missed them. We can't have been far behind, though. At least we stopped them setting fire to the truck.'

'Oh?'

'There wasn't much diesel in the tank, which meant that they struggled to reach it with the bits of cloth they were using. They heard our sirens. So they gave up and scarpered.'

'Across the dunes?'

'Probably.'

Well away by now, then. Still, the news was pretty good. They had lost their transport and were in disarray. The tide had turned.

'You should be able to get a lot of information from the truck.'

Bill nodded. 'That's what we're counting on. Forensics are taking it apart right now. If I'd had my way, they'd have been working overnight, but . . . '

He didn't finish the sentence.

'But budget cuts?' I finished for him.

He nodded. 'Overtime working cut right back. Still, we should hear something today.'

It was good news. Bill might know who he was looking for then, which would get them off my back.

'I can tell you one thing right now, though,' Bill said quietly. 'I doubt if those men killed James Campbell.'

'Oh? Why's that?'

'Forensics established that he was killed some time before being put into the water. My guess is that the three toughs you saw at the Gare were just a disposal team.'

Interesting. That could answer a few questions. The Geordies hadn't seemed like a proper hit team. Too rough and ready for that, and they were doing stupid things. It was as if they had panicked after being seen at the Gare that day. It had surprised me all along that McCardle hadn't been able to find better quality. Perhaps he had.

'So there might have been someone else?' I said thoughtfully.

Bill nodded. 'Not necessarily a hit man,

though,' he added. 'Campbell's death could just have been an unfortunate accident, leaving someone with a body to dispose of.'

It was a possibility. But not a strong one. I knew that really we were both thinking of the guy I'd tumbled off the cliff.

'James was still killed,' Nancy said, stung into making a contribution.

'Yes, indeed,' Bill said, nodding. 'Nobody is questioning that.'

★　★　★

Later, I turned on the computer to check my emails. I knew instantly that someone had been there before me. There was an unopened message from a double-glazing firm in my inbox that I had not brought down from the server.

Had Nancy been on the computer? I was pretty sure she hadn't. There hadn't been time. The man I'd killed? Nope. I'd looked at my emails since he went off the cliff, and this message hadn't been there then.

Someone else then?

I shrugged. That wasn't a question I could answer.

I put the computer on standby. Time was pressing. We still had to sort out what we were going to do about PortPlus.

My idea was to take the fight to them. Nancy was receptive, but puzzled.

'How can we do that?'

'We can start by undermining their credibility. I'm going to talk to people, people who matter.'

She looked doubtful. 'Like who?'

'The press, the council and anyone else we can think of. We've got to start somewhere.'

'What about me? Where do I fit in?'

It was the opportunity I'd been waiting for.

'That's easy,' I said. 'You can start by telling me what you know about McCardle, and about James' involvement with him. You've not done that so far.'

She gave me an uneasy, rueful smile. 'I forgot,' she said.

I smiled back at her. 'Of course you did,' I said.

'What do you want to know?' she asked. 'What can I tell you?'

'Start with McCardle. What do you know about him?'

We were sat at the kitchen table. Nancy was fidgety, as if she would rather have been doing something else. So would I, but I needed to make progress.

'Donovan McCardle is James' brother.'

I stared at her, shocked. I hadn't seen that one coming. 'Are you sure?'

She nodded. 'He's a lot older than James was, of course. Their mother had Donovan when she was very young.'

'Where was this?'

'South Africa. Later, after her husband died, she remarried and moved with James to Zimbabwe. Donovan didn't go with them. He had left home by then, and had changed his name for some reason. He was busy building a business career.'

She looked at me, shrugged and added, 'James didn't approve of Donovan.'

'Why not?'

'The name change was one thing. Then his career was in mining, and in Africa that usually means exploitation. Big profits, terrible conditions for the workers, violent camps, and so on. James didn't like that. He was different.'

She got up and switched the kettle on. 'More coffee?'

'Thank you. But that's usually my job.'

'I'm working my passage.' She smiled and continued. 'The brothers had nothing to do with each other for many years. Then they met again in London, at a big business conference. By then, James was living here, and was an MP. Donovan had just lost his platinum mine in Zimbabwe and was looking for new business opportunities.'

'Oh, yes. The mines were nationalized, weren't they? Henry told me.'

She shrugged, as if to say that was one way of looking at it. Perhaps expropriated was a better way.

'Anyway, they talked, got on quite well, and James somehow sold Donovan the idea that there were big business opportunities on Teesside, big investment opportunities.'

'And that's how it all started?'

She nodded. 'Donovan came here, looked around and decided to take over the port and do various other things. It was those other things that led to James changing his mind. He didn't like them, and soon decided he couldn't support them.'

'A serious difference of opinion?'

'Very. James told me he would tell Donovan that he would campaign against the PortPlus project. That's when all this started — and that's all I know.'

I nodded. 'What you've just told me explains a lot.'

Campbell had signed his own death warrant, in effect. Brother or not, McCardle or his associates had not been prepared to let him sink their project. Money had been spent already, and more was being risked. Coming after losing so much in Africa, failure had been unthinkable. So James had to go.

'There is one thing I don't understand,' I said. 'Was McCardle expecting to make a lot of money out of running the port?'

'No, I don't think so. He wanted the land the port owns. James said the big money was going to come out of new housing development. Once they got approval for that, they would make their money fast and get out.'

I nodded. It made sense. Almost.

'Who did they think would buy all the new houses? This isn't an affluent part of the country.'

'People would come here, they believed. They would effectively build a new town on the waterside, and people would come.'

'With our climate and our industrial history?'

She shrugged.

Maybe, I thought. It was certainly a bold idea. Would it work, though? Not if I could help it!

'We're going to stop them,' I said grimly.

'How?'

'We'll find a way.'

She came close and wrapped her arms around me. 'My man!' she said.

29

With Nancy's help, I persuaded Jack Gregory to arrange a meeting with the leader of Redcar and Cleveland Borough Council, a man belonging to the same party as James Campbell. It wasn't easy, I gathered.

'I've done it,' Jack said, 'but I don't think you'll get a very friendly ear. Michael Donnelly is eager to bring in PortPlus. So watch yourself!'

'But he's granted me an audience anyway?'

'Oh yes!' Jack chuckled cynically. 'He wants the party's nomination to replace James. He can't afford to alienate anyone at this stage.'

'Especially the party's constituency agent?'

'Well . . . ' He paused and gave me a grin. 'He was no friend of James', or, by association, of me either. If he could have worked it, he would have had James deselected. But there was no chance of that happening. So he had to keep his powder dry. For the moment, at least, he's still doing that.'

'Is your job in jeopardy now James has gone?'

'I would think so, wouldn't you? Not many constituency parties have an agent any more anyway. So he'll probably move quickly to get my post abolished as a cost-saving move.'

He gave a little chuckle, sounding amused. 'You're not worried?'

He was even more amused now. 'Frank, this is politics! It's what we live for. 'The king is dead, long live the king!', and all that.'

I laughed and shook my head. 'You sound about as secure in your job as I am in mine,' I told him.

'Maybe,' he said, 'but something always turns up, doesn't it?'

★ ★ ★

I met Michael Donnelly in the leader's office in Normanby Road, Eston. He was a large, easy-going seeming man. Although he was of Irish descent — from Sligo, he soon let me know — his accent was pure Middlesbrough. No doubt he had paid visits to the ancestral homeland, like Barack Obama and Bill Clinton, but I was willing to bet his father and grand-father, and probably even his great-grandfather, had all been born in Middlesbrough. In my view, you vote with your feet, and home is where you hang your hat.

'Come in, come in, Frank!' he cried, emerging from behind his vast desk to greet me.

I nodded and smiled, and thanked him for agreeing to see me.

'When a good friend like Jack Gregory asks for a favour, especially at such a sad time as this, I am not the man to turn him away. Of course I'm happy to see you!'

He was secure enough in his party and local standing to have given me the brush-off, of course, but already he was running for a different office. He couldn't afford to antagonize Jack Gregory and all the other people who had believed in James Campbell. Not yet anyway. That would no doubt happen when he had the votes in the bag. Given his current standing, I didn't suppose that would take too long.

To get anywhere with my hopes of undermining PortPlus, I knew I had to hit hard and early in the political world. So I told him how I had become involved in the James Campbell tragedy, and then went on to state my case against PortPlus. They were a bunch of charlatans, I concluded, and possibly worse.

Unfortunately, my case was mostly suspicion, innuendo and rumour, backed up by the knowledge that James Campbell himself had been about to campaign against them. I added to that the fact that McCardle's background was in African mining, and that as far as anyone had been able to discover, PortPlus had no experience of port management.

Donnelly listened intently and without interruption. But the cogs in his head were whirring. I could hear them, and I could sense the judgements he was shaping and the decisions he was coming to long before I finished. I was reluctantly impressed. The man was no pushover.

When I was done, he poured two cups of coffee from a waiting flask and set them on the little table between us, along with bowls of sugar and milk.

'I understand how you got sucked into all this, Frank,' he said. 'You were enjoying a pleasant afternoon by the sea, and became the unfortunate bystander that just happens to get hit by a ricochet. Collateral damage, yes?'

'Something like that.'

'And then you were pursued by evil men as a consequence, men who were afraid you would be able to identify them.' He nodded to himself, as if satisfied that he had summed up the starting situation perfectly, as indeed he had. Then he moved on to what happened next.

'If there is any way I can help bring pressure on the police service to provide protection, you must let me know. The Chief Constable is a very good friend of mine. Indeed,' he added with a wry smile, 'I played some small part in his appointment.'

That was no surprise to me. I was sure it wouldn't have been news to Bill Peart either. Even though we don't yet have elections for police chiefs, chief constables have always been political appointments made by people — men mostly — in what used to be smoke-filled rooms. I doubt if the new police commissioners will change that.

'However,' he continued, a frown beginning to appear, 'this business about PortPlus is a different matter. I believe it to be entirely unconnected to James Campbell's unfortunate demise. There is no evidence that says otherwise. And I must tell you, PortPlus have offered a vision for the future of this area that is unrivalled. Never in our wildest dreams could we have hoped for inward investment and regeneration on the scale they are proposing.'

He shrugged and added, 'So this council supports them and what they want to do. As do government ministers, I might add, and the vast majority of our citizens. The current port operators do not, of course,' he added with an understanding smile.

'Maybe you should listen to the Teesport

people,' I said doggedly. 'They're in the business, and have been for a long time. They know what they're talking about.'

'As do PortPlus.'

'Do they, though? Where has their experience come from? I haven't been able to find any evidence of them running a port anywhere in the world.'

'They are involved in many, many ports. Maputo, for one, in Mozambique. Ports in the United States for another.'

'But not as principals. They might have a financial interest, although that doesn't appear publicly, but they don't actually run a port.'

'They will! They will soon.' He smiled at me infuriatingly. 'I think you underestimate PortPlus.'

'On the contrary, I've met McCardle and his sidekick Rogers. I know what they're like. I also know that James Campbell had decided they were no good for Teesport or this area, and was about to campaign against them. He had good reason.'

Donnelly nodded and paused. 'Was there anything else?' he asked a moment or two later.

Clearly, that last card had not played well. I considered for a moment, and then decided I was in it up to my neck anyway. Why not go for broke?

'Off the record, I want to ask you to consider that PortPlus might be a front operation only. Their so-called HQ turned out to be a vacant office in Middlesbrough they had rented for a week. They told the agency they wanted it for promotional purposes. There's nothing behind the front. And now they've moved to different premises.

'Somehow,' I added, 'McCardle is in this to make quick money to replace what he lost in Zimbabwe when his mining business was expropriated. I'm not yet sure how he intends doing that, but you can bet there's no way he's interested in running a port in the long term. PortPlus will probably asset strip, not do the good things they promised, and then move on, having turned a quick buck.'

I could see from Donnelly's expression that my diatribe had not gone down well.

'Mr Doy,' he said in a less friendly tone, 'I have given you a lot of my time this morning. I have sat here and listened patiently to what you had to say, and I have to tell you it's a load of horse manure. Now I would be grateful if you would leave me to get on with my job. I have another appointment coming up.'

So that had gone well, I thought, on the way out. I hadn't laid a glove on him — or on PortPlus.

30

'How did you get on?' Nancy asked when I got back to the car.

'Don't ask!'

'That bad?'

'Worse. What makes it worse is the man's pretty astute. He's nobody's fool.'

'Why is that worse?'

'He knows what he's doing. He's no innocent. So maybe we're wrong, and James Campbell was wrong too.'

'But you don't think so?'

I shook my head. I didn't think we were wrong. My instincts said we were right. Port-Plus were a charade, and McCardle and Rogers international con men, if not mobsters. Otherwise, there was too much to explain.

I couldn't see James Campbell's murder, just as he was about to launch his anti-PortPlus campaign, as a coincidence. Then there was the job offer to me, and the attacks that had redoubled since I declined it.

What I couldn't explain was how PortPlus had pulled the wool over Donnelly's eyes. They didn't operate a port anywhere! Why couldn't Donnelly see that?

'What else did you think of him?' Nancy pressed.

'He's a Middlesbrough man, pretending to be Irish.'

'So?'

'I didn't like him. He's an insincere, nasty piece of work — but capable and powerful.'

'Corrupt?'

I just shrugged. I had no idea. It was certainly a possibility, though.

I mulled it over. Corruption could explain why Donnelly was so supportive of PortPlus, although it would be hard to pull off these days, given the structure of local government, and all the checks and balances. One man could still be paid backhanders, I supposed, but even the leader of a council couldn't take decisions unilaterally. Influence them, certainly, but not take them. There wouldn't be much money in that.

My feeling was that Donnelly probably wasn't on the take. He was just one of many who for some reason saw PortPlus as the potential saviour for the area. If he was right, his career would get a big boost. So . . . Mistaken, perhaps, but not necessarily corrupt.

'Maybe he's supportive of PortPlus just because James had turned against them?' Nancy suggested.

'I would buy that if James had been

campaigning for some time, but he hadn't, had he?'

Nancy shook her head and sighed. 'What now?' she asked.

'I'm going to talk to someone else.'

'Can you run me home first? I've got things to do.'

'Do you want to come back with me afterwards?'

'Tomorrow, Frank. Pick me up tomorrow.'

I didn't like that idea. The Geordies were still around, and she was still vulnerable.

'Sure?'

She nodded firmly. 'I'm not going to shelter under your wing, Frank. I need to stand up for myself. No-one is going to frighten me out of my own home.'

'OK,' I said reluctantly, giving her a hug. 'But take care.'

★　★　★

I phoned the *Evening Gazette* and asked for Colin Ryder, the reporter who had covered the PortPlus launch, and asked to meet him. He was cautious.

'What about?' he wanted to know.

'PortPlus,' I said. 'I don't believe they're genuine.'

He chuckled. 'I've heard that before. What

makes you think it?'

'For one thing, I know James Campbell was opposed to their takeover bid, and he was murdered. For another, I can find no evidence that they have ever been involved in operating a port.'

'So what, if they can do it?'

'There's a question of credibility surely? Their background is in African mining — until they got chucked out.'

'So they've changed course. McCardle isn't stupid, you know. He believes they can make it work.'

'He's just hoping to make a pile of money fast!'

'That's what makes the world go round. Unless you've got anything specific against him, Mr Doy, I don't think I can spare the time to meet you right now.'

'When the full story comes out,' I said bitterly, 'you'll be sorry you missed it.'

'No doubt. By the way, you do know Redcar and Cleveland Council has given its full backing to PortPlus, and Middlesbrough is inclined to do the same?'

'They're all desperate.'

'So are a lot of the people PortPlus are promising to help with jobs and houses. Besides, the politicians have examined the proposals in detail. They think they're viable.'

'Yeah?'

'Get something new, and I'll talk to you again. Cheers.'

So that had gone as well as the meeting with Donnelly, I thought afterwards, feeling morose. What was wrong with them all? Maybe I was just no good at explaining myself.

★ ★ ★

Bill Peart was waiting for me when I got back to Risky Point. I wasn't at all sure he was who I wanted to see right then, but I had to let him inside and go through the motions of being hospitable.

'I've just been talking to Jimmy Mack,' he volunteered. 'Interesting man, that.'

'He's an old windbag,' I said sourly.

'No, no! I wouldn't say that. It's surprising what he knows. I often learn a lot from him.'

As I put the kettle on, I wondered where this was going. I was used to Bill's crafty introductions. Either there was something he wanted from me or he'd caught a whiff of something that he could hold against me. Bloody Jimmy! What had he been saying now?

I made a pot of tea and let it brew, while Bill prattled on about the fish he was hoping to catch when next he found some time to come down here and get me and Jimmy to take him out in the boat.

'Tea?' he said, as I poured it out.

'No coffee left, and I forgot to get some more.'

'All the women that pass through your door,' he grumbled, 'and you can't get one of them to see to the grocery order?'

'They're guests, Bill, not cheap domestics.'

'If you say so. And this latest one lives in a shed at the South Gare, I hear?'

Bloody Jimmy again!

'She has a fisherman's hut there. It was her grandfather's.'

'I wasn't aware that those sheds — huts, sorry — were suitable for permanent accommodation?'

I yawned. 'What was it you wanted, Bill? I've had a rotten day so far.'

'Too many late nights? Oh, well. You'll learn. We all have to go through that stage in life, I suppose.'

I shook my head and chuckled without feeling amused. 'You workaholics! You're all the same. You think life is about stopping everyone else enjoying themselves.'

'You're confusing me with the tax man,' Bill said equably. 'I just think you should stay away from the South Gare, and from Port-Plus.'

'You do, eh?'

He nodded.

'Any reason?'

'None that I can disclose.'

That meant he had nothing. He just didn't want me interfering, as he would see it. He just wanted me to be here when he needed to ask me questions.

'How's the murder investigation going?'

'Not well. We haven't a clue who shot Campbell. But it wasn't the Geordie lads.'

'Really? Have you found them, and asked them?'

'Not yet. But we will.'

'And the other inquiry? The guy who attacked me, and then fell off the cliff?'

He shook his head. 'No body found yet.'

He looked at me speculatively.

'It did happen, Bill, if that's what you're wondering!'

He grinned and nodded.

'This tea,' he said, swilling it round with a spoon. 'A bit weak, isn't it?'

'It's an art,' I admitted, 'one I haven't mastered yet.'

I made more. We watched the pot while the tea brewed.

'Coffee's a lot easier,' Bill said. 'And quicker.'

'Perhaps you could bring some next time you come?'

He grinned again. Then he said in a

conversational tone, 'I have to be careful, Frank. So do you. The Chief has taken his line from the politicians, and he doesn't want to hear any whispers about PortPlus. So far as he's concerned, what PortPlus want to do is a grand thing. He's all for it — and for them.'

'Why do I have to be careful?'

'He's been receiving complaints about you getting in the way, wasting folks' time and so on. He wonders if you're a credible witness for what you say you saw at the Gare that day. He wants me to find out if you might have been involved yourself in Campbell's murder.'

I stared with disbelief and shook my head. 'That's absolutely stupid!'

He nodded. 'I agree. But it's the world we live in, unfortunately.'

'So you're telling me to back off?'

'Not exactly. I'm telling you you're not flavour of the month in certain quarters, and to watch your back.'

'Thank you!'

'There's another thing.'

'What's that?'

'I'm not sure about this, but whoever shot Campbell might still be around. It wasn't necessarily the guy who fell off the cliff. Anyway, I wouldn't want him — or her, or them — to think you might be a danger to them. So watch yourself.'

31

The larder was looking bare. Two people eat more than one, I suppose. So I called into the big supermarket in Redcar and started filling my trolley with a mix of stuff that's good for you and stuff that I like. I didn't bother speculating about Nancy's preferences. She seemed to eat anything that came her way, probably due to advanced poverty.

That thought made me smile. It wasn't often I came across easy-to-please women where food was concerned.

Then I came face to face with Jac Picknett at the cheese counter.

'You're back!' I said as soon as surprise allowed.

'Hello, Frank. Yes, I'm back.'

'How are you?'

'I'm fine, thanks. You?'

She seemed less surprised than me, perhaps because she had known she was back, and that I had never gone away.

'I'm OK, thanks.'

It was a bit awkward, the two of us standing there as if we hardly knew each other, and I suppose it had slipped my mind that our last meeting had ended the way it had.

'Look, do you fancy a coffee?'

'I don't think so, Frank. I'm rather busy.'

I nodded. 'Me, too. What about getting together for a meal? I need to bring you up to date.'

She gave me a wan smile. 'Better not. I meant what I said last time we met, Frank.'

I had recalled her words by then, and now I gave her a rueful smile.

'Besides,' she added, 'I've met someone. You and I had our time, Frank. Let's leave it at that.'

I nodded, thinking to myself that at least I didn't have to make up any explanations about Nancy.

'You've met someone? Good. Anyone I know?'

She shook her head firmly. 'No chance of that. He's American, and hasn't been here long. He just happened to come into the gallery one day, and . . . Well, there you are!'

There, indeed. Fast work. Well, good luck to her. She was every bit as free as I was myself.

'Oh, there is one thing!' I said, a thought coming to mind belatedly. 'If I email you photos of a couple of paintings, would you mind answering a question or two about them

— giving me your expert opinion?'

She smiled.

'Basically,' I added, 'I'd like to know if they're worth anything.'

'I can hardly tell from photos, Frank.'

'If they're what I think they might be, you can see them for yourself. But I don't want to waste your time.'

'All right. Send the photos.'

We nodded politely and parted. People who once had known each other. Like that.

★ ★ ★

I loaded up the Mondeo estate Eric had loaned me, left the car park and parked in a quiet street. Then I headed for the Lord Zetland, where I was unlikely to see anyone who knew me, to see what their guest ales were that week. I needed to sit quietly and think. Bumping into Jac had been a surprise, a shock really. For a time, I had assumed we were long-term, if not permanent, as a couple. I'd certainly got that wrong.

Distracted as I was, I walked right into it.

It's a very basic old pub, the Lord Zetland. A narrow corridor runs from the front door through to the toilets at the back. To the right is a staircase to the unused, upper part of the building. To the left are the doors to the bar, the snug and the lounge.

I was halfway along the corridor when the door to the Gents opened and out came one of the three Geordies. I saw him before he saw me. I spun round, and was just in time to come face to face with the main man emerging from the bar. He was a few feet from me, and even more surprised than I was.

I made use of my micro-second advantage. Before he had registered who I was, I slammed a punch to his belly that doubled him up. Then I caught him by the collar and ran with him to slam his head into the opposite wall. He went down like a popped crisp bag.

The guy from the Gents was on me by then. I dropped low to evade his fist, seized him round the thighs and straightened up to heave him over my shoulder. He landed awkwardly with a scream, and stayed down.

I went back to work then on the leader, giving him a hammering that was revenge for all the threats and all the damage he'd done to me. Sheer blood lust. It took three men to pull me off him. By then he was no longer moving much, and his face was a bloody mess.

'Hold him!' a man I knew to be the landlord shouted. 'I've called the police.'

I began to calm down. The landlord had done exactly what I would have wanted him to do.

'Where's the other one?' I panted at the big, burly bloke who had me in a headlock. 'There were three of them. They were together.'

'You've done enough damage!' he growled. 'You don't need no more.'

'You can let go of me,' I said. 'It's over.'

'It soon will be,' he said. 'The cops will be here any minute.'

'That's fine, exactly what I want. The police want the three of them.'

'Yeah, yeah!'

But they chuckled and let go of me. Then they started raising the leader of the pack from the floor. He was coming round by then, but he wasn't in great shape.

I got my phone out and called Bill Peart to tell him who I had found. I said I was being held, and was worried the Geordies would get away.

'Put the landlord on,' Bill snapped.

I handed over the phone. 'Detective Inspector Peart wants to speak to you,' I said. 'And I've just made a citizen's arrest.'

He gaped at me as if he thought I was crazy. Perhaps I was still. But he talked to Bill. After that, things got easier for me. The landlord and his mates turned their attention to the two men I had beaten up. I had no idea where the third one was.

* * *

Afterwards, Bill took me away in his vehicle. He parked on the sea front and debriefed me.

'We've got the two of them,' he said. 'We know now who they are. Just some Geordie low-life from the east end of Newcastle.'

I nodded.

'How are you feeling?' he added, giving me a cautious glance.

'Never better,' I assured him.

'It didn't occur to you to give me a call, and stay out of it yourself?'

I shook my head. 'There was no time, Bill! We just bumped into each other in that passage in the pub. Then it was them or me, whoever reacted first. You've seen what it's like in there!'

'Yeah.' He yawned and stretched. 'It's been a long day. You did well,' he added, 'but I still might have to arrest you at some point.'

'Whatever,' I said with a shrug. 'I'm just happy they're off the street at last. Two of them, anyway.'

'We'll find the other one. He'll not get far on his own.'

There wasn't a lot more to talk about. I had him run me back to where I'd parked my car.

'It's not over,' he said as a parting shot. 'Those three are not the ones you need to worry about. You do know that?'

I grinned at him and said, 'I already dealt with the real hit man, remember?'

I shut the door and he drove off, worrying again, like he always did.

Me? I felt light as a feather. My aching hands told me I'd given a good account of myself, and I had a bit less to worry about now. If only PortPlus could be dealt with so satisfactorily.

32

The Save-our-Seals people had a hut on the edge of what was left of the marshes around Seal Sands. When I visited them, I met a man and a woman who were doing their best to field phone calls, send out appeals for funds, provide anyone who showed up with information, and keep the kettle boiling for tea.

Brian Smith was an early-retired teacher who introduced himself as the chair of Save Our Seals. Alison Reddy, a friendly middle-aged activist, was the treasurer. I accepted a mug of tea from her gratefully.

Brian asked me what my interest was, and I decided not to beat around the bush.

'I want to do everything I can to stop PortPlus,' I told him. 'I think they're a bunch of cowboys who will do Teesside no good, whatever the politicians and the people desperate for jobs might think. They're here to make a fast buck, and then clear out. Besides,' I added, 'I like seals.'

Alison hooted with delight and Brian said, 'You're our kind of person, Frank!'

I had arranged to visit them because so far

I had gathered very little information about the ecological side of things. They were eager to talk to me.

'It would be a disaster if we lost the seals, not that that's going to happen,' Brian said. 'Before industrialization the native colony of Common Seals had been here since time immemorial. It did die out in the nineteenth century, but twenty years ago it restarted and now it's thriving again.'

'We have Grey Seals from the Farne Islands as well, now,' Alison added.

I sipped my coffee. It was even worse than what I make, but I tried not to show it.

'What's to stop PortPlus getting rid of them all?' I asked.

Brian chuckled. 'How could they do that?'

'Well, by deterring them from coming, for example? Or by introducing a virus to kill them off?'

'We would be onto them like a ton of bricks,' Alison said.

Brian shook his head. 'It's too far-fetched. It's not going to happen.'

On reflection, Alison was a bit less adamant. 'I suppose, theoretically, they could make life so uncomfortable for them that it stopped them breeding and made them leave.'

'But how could they do that?' Brian asked again.

'By using low-level sound, for example?' She shrugged. 'It is possible, isn't it?'

Brian was unhappy now and restless. He got up from the table and walked over to the window. He leaned against the sill and stared out at the marsh grass, and the petrochemical complex not far beyond.

'I'm uncomfortable with this,' he said over his shoulder. 'I know you mean well, Frank, but I don't believe any reputable company would resort to anything like that in this day and age.'

'Reputable company?' I mused. 'Is that what PortPlus is? I can't find anything about them.'

I didn't get much further with Brian and Alison. They were decent people spending time and money on something they believed to be important. They were concerned about the rumours flying around, but not seriously worried. Nor was I by then, not in relation to the seals. The general air of uncertainty PortPlus had created was more worrying.

★ ★ ★

More pressing than the seals were questions to do with money. It was time I saw Henry again.

I asked him outright how PortPlus were

going to make serious money out of the takeover, if it went ahead.

'It's not rocket science,' Henry said with a shrug. 'There's no big mystery.'

'No?'

'The actual port operation is profitable right now, and a change of ownership won't affect that. New owners could keep most of the top management, and just tell them to keep on doing what they've been doing.'

'No change there, then?'

'None at all, unless they want to make some.'

'So what will they do that is different? Build this nuclear power station I keep hearing about?'

Henry shook his head. 'I don't think so.'

'Come on, Henry! I'm busy.'

'Think about it. How have most big fortunes been made in the last few decades?'

'If I knew, Henry, I'd be doing it myself! How? Shopping malls?'

'Housing. New houses. Sure, developers build shopping malls and recreation centres, industrial estates and sports centres, but new houses are the big profit makers. It's one area of the economy where growth in demand is relentless. With sustained immigration and population growth, as well as people wanting ever bigger homes, that's unlikely to change as far ahead as I can see. My guess is PortPlus will build a lot of executive-style, waterfront houses all around the estuary. Then they'll sell them and move on. Once they've made their money out of the houses, they'll flog the port. That's just a means to an end.'

It was the same picture Nancy had painted, and perhaps it was what James Campbell had feared. But was it a true picture? I still couldn't see it somehow.

'Are you sure, Henry? I mean, what about the newly reopened steelworks? Won't that be a spanner in the works? You can't build houses near a blast furnace. Not any more!'

Henry chuckled. 'The one blast furnace left on Teesside? How long do you think that's going to last, Frank? Teesside is no longer a viable location for steel making.'

'The new owners must think it is. They've spent a lot on the Redcar plant.'

'Foreign owners, though. Some Chinese or Indian steel company will come along and make them an offer they can't refuse. They'll buy it, and then shut it down for good to reduce the competition. It's happened often enough before, in different industries. Then the way will be clear to build a new waterfront town for people who like messing about in boats.'

It was a depressing scenario. Local people had believed their future was secure when foreign owners took over and reopened Teesside's last steelworks, but the picture Henry had sketched was pretty plausible. We had seen it before. He was right.

Mind you, building a new town on the edge of the sea was not an altogether unattractive idea. Get rid of all the clutter and dereliction, and make better use of the location? What was wrong with that?

Well, Nancy and the other fishermen would lose their huts at the South Gare, for one. And then McCardle and his cronies would walk away with a pile of money, for another — and murder would go unpunished. I didn't want any of that. I couldn't save the world but I wasn't about to give up on the things I could do something about.

★ ★ ★

Arriving back at Risky Point, I was suddenly uneasy. I couldn't put my finger on it, but something felt wrong. I stood beside the car and looked around. Nothing. I could hear and see nothing out of the ordinary. Not even any of the rabbits that Jimmy Mack and I were forever chasing away from our feeble attempts to grow vegetables. It was quiet, too. Even the sea seemed unusually quiet.

I felt watched. I had that prickly feeling I'd had before, more than once, lately. I gave a mental shrug and went inside. I didn't find signs of an intruder this time, but that didn't mean no-one had been here. I wasn't reassured. I still felt watched — and threatened.

★   ★   ★

I wasn't always pleased to see Bill Peart arriving at my door, but that day it was different. I needed a familiar, friendly face and someone to talk to about ordinary things, like whether the fish would be running.

'I'm glad I caught you in,' he said, as if he had been calling every day for a month and never yet managed to find me at home.

'There's still no coffee,' I said flatly. 'You'll have to have tea again.'

'Still no coffee? What happened to your latest woman?'

'Nancy, you mean? I've got news for you, Bill. Modern young women don't do the shopping any more. So men like me have to do it ourselves.'

'Oh? Like that, is it? Tea, then. Two sugars.'

We took our mugs outside and sat in the sun around a driftwood table I had made from tree stumps that had washed up on the beach. It rocked a bit, but it did the job.

'This is something you could do,' Bill said, gently testing the table.

'To make an honest living, you mean?'

'Exactly. Make a few more of these, and you'll soon get the hang of it.'

'I'll think about it.'

He grinned. 'It's not a bad day, is it?' he said, raising his face to the sky. 'Is that the sun up there?'

'I believe it is. Make the most of it.'

'How are you feeling?' he asked suddenly.

'OK. Why?'

'Well, things have been happening to you,' he said with a shrug. 'First here, and then that business in the Lord Zetland. Sometimes the stress doesn't appear for a while.'

Bill in counsellor mode. In some ways it was worse than Bill in critical mode.

'I'm really OK, Bill. But thanks for the concern.'

He nodded and inspected his mug. I realized then that there was more to come. He just wasn't finding it easy to get round to it, whatever it was.

'What about the Geordies?' I asked. 'Did you find the third man?'

'We did. He wasn't far away. We picked him up on the sea front. He was lost without Jack

Morgan to tell him what to do.'

'Morgan is leader of the pack?'

Bill nodded. 'By the way, he's confirmed what I suspected. It wasn't them that shot Campbell. They were just told to get rid of the body.'

'Who told them to do that?'

'He's not saying yet, but he will. There's no way he's going to accept a murder rap.'

'So when they came looking for me, they just wanted to slap me about a bit to frighten me? They weren't going to kill me, or do anything really nasty?'

'Who knows how far it would have gone? What they wanted was to stop you identifying them, and putting them in the frame for the murder.'

That sounded about right to me. But, as Bill said, who could say how far they would have gone?

'Did they tell you who did kill Campbell?'

Bill nodded. 'It seems to have been the guy you took care of on the cliff. They didn't have a name for him, but that's what it looks like. He was a professional hitman.'

No surprise there. The man had come for me with a gun.

'Hired by PortPlus?'

'You can't say that, Frank! You know you can't. And neither can I.'

231

His heart wasn't in it, though. I could tell. He did his best to stay within the rules and procedures, not to mention the law itself, but at times it was hard for him.

'We found the body,' he added. 'Eventually.'

'Oh?'

'A couple of miles down the coast, near Port Holland. Two blokes digging for bait saw it washing around in the shallows. After they'd got it out, and stopped vomiting, they gave us a call.'

'Any ID?'

He shook his head. 'But we know now who it was. The FBI told us.'

'Really? So he was American?'

Bill nodded and looked up at me. 'He was a top man, apparently, with a string of hits to his name. The FBI had got close to him, which is why he'd started operating overseas.'

'Lucky us!'

'Quite.' Bill paused and then added, 'He was good, Frank, really good. You did well to handle him.'

I shrugged. 'He made mistakes, and I got lucky.'

Bill nodded and took a swig of tea. Then we discussed the recent weather and what it might mean for fishing down this coast. I told him Jimmy Mack reckoned it would be good in a week or two's time, when the seas settled down again.

'I'll grab a bit of leave, and we can see if he's right?' Bill suggested.

'Good idea.'

A big gull landed nearby on the garden wall. I fed him a chunk of bread. He took it, but seemed unimpressed by the meagre offering.

'They like fish and chips best,' Bill said. 'I've seen them in Whitby, hanging around on the pavement outside the chip shops.'

'He'd better hurry back there, then. There's nothing like that here.'

Bill nodded. He seemed subdued, still something more on his mind.

'It's not over,' he said suddenly. 'You do know that, don't you?'

'What isn't? The business with PortPlus?'

'I'm not thinking of that. This hit man, name of Ronnie Garcia. He always works with a partner, or he did.'

That brought my head round.

'Even overseas?'

Bill nodded. 'So they say, the FBI. Guy called Sal.'

'Italian?'

'Possibly. I don't know.'

I chewed my lip for a moment. This was unexpected. Yet it sounded right. It could explain the feeling of being watched I'd had so much lately. One or two other little mysteries, as well.

'And you think he's still around?'

'I do. So do the FBI. They say this Sal will come looking for you, especially now.'

'Well, I'm not going anywhere. I can deal with it better here than anywhere else.'

'I thought you'd say something stupid like that,' Bill said bitterly. He pushed his chair back. 'Let me know if you need anything. I'll be around.'

'Thanks for letting me know.'

'Couldn't avoid it,' he said. 'There's no-one else for me to go fishing with.'

33

Jac Picknett rang, wanting to know where I had seen the pictures I had emailed her about.

'At this stage, Jac, I can't tell you.'

She had backed out of my life — for reasons I could understand and agreed with — and I didn't want her coming back in, not inadvertently anyway. There was enough going on without me having to worry about her safety.

'That's a pity.' She hesitated and then added, 'It's just that I've seen those pictures myself. Somebody showed me them.'

'Really?'

I wondered who that had been, but didn't ask. I waited but she didn't add anything. I sensed that there was something she couldn't bring herself to tell me. Well, I wasn't going to force or cajole her.

'Is there any chance at all that they are real?'

She chuckled. 'Real Turners, you mean?'

There! She'd come out with the name I had been avoiding uttering, even to myself, and certainly not to Nancy.

'That's exactly what I mean.'

'I hate to disappoint you, Frank, but . . . no. I really don't think so. Not unless you have been to California recently, and visited the Getty Museum.'

'Is that where the originals are?'

'Indeed. They're worth millions.'

Oh, well. I hadn't mentioned my thoughts to Nancy. So she couldn't be disappointed now.

'The third picture is a different matter,' Jac added. 'That could be an original. It probably is, in fact.'

'Original what?'

'An original Grimshaw.'

'Oh, good! An original Grimshaw? Thank you very much for that, Jac.'

She laughed and rang off.

Possibly an original Grimshaw. I didn't think I would bother Nancy with that bit of news either. She needed something to cheer her up.

★　★　★

The phone rang again. I picked it up.

'I'm coming for you, Doy. I'm coming for you.'

It was a startling announcement, delivered in a strange, mechanical voice.

'Who is this? The disguised voice doesn't impress me, by the way.'

'You won't see me, but I'm here,' the voice droned.

It was like listening to Stephen Hawking.

'Give me a clue.'

'You killed my partner. Now I'm coming for you.'

The phone went dead.

Sal? Was that the name Bill had mentioned?

I put the phone down and stared thoughtfully out of the kitchen window. Was he here already? Someone was, watching me and going through my house when I was out. Sal? It had to be.

What to do about it? I couldn't just ignore the message. On the other hand, I wasn't going to run around in a panic either. That would be what he wanted.

He would be armed. So I needed to be, too. I took out the old Glock pistol I kept hidden away. I cleaned it and made sure it was working smoothly. Only very occasionally did I have a use for it — usually when I went abroad — but there was no way I was going to risk coming up against another professional hitman without it.

Then it was time to hit the road. I had things to do. One of them was to recce the new PortPlus HQ. Somehow I had to go on the offensive, and I couldn't think of a better place or way to start.

★ ★ ★

Sutton Castle was where PortPlus now had their corporate headquarters. It wasn't a real castle; more a posh Victorian house at the centre of a big rural estate. It was on the edge of the Cleveland Hills, set in rolling parkland that spoke of a pre-industrial history.

PortPlus would have leased the place, no doubt for a bit longer than the week for which they had occupied Riverside House. From this location, they could see a lot of that which they aspired to own: the lower Tees valley, and all it contained.

I turned off the main road and drove up a narrow lane to the main entrance. The big, ornamental gates were open. I drove through, and on past a belt of dense rhododendron and huge pine trees. An impressive approach.

The access road terminated in a large car park to one side of the house. A few cars were parked there. A couple of Mercedes and BMWs, plus one or two lesser vehicles. The house itself was all turrets and fancy chimney stacks, a piece of elaborate Victoriana.

Not much was happening. In fact, nothing at all. So much for frantic financial manoeuvrings. Presumably all that was being done via conference calls and the World Wide Web.

As I turned the car round and headed back out, I wondered yet again where the money for the takeover was coming from. Borrowed, probably. So much, though? I wouldn't want to be the one paying the interest charges. McCardle had plenty of nerve.

*   *   *

I slowed down, turned on to the track leading to Risky Point and began the careful negotiation of the potholes and craters that hindered the approach to the cottages. Ordinarily, in my old Land Rover, I wouldn't have bothered being so careful, but this was Eric's car, not mine. I didn't want him complaining when I handed it back.

Halfway along the track, something whizzed through the open window. The windscreen suddenly became opaque as myriad cracks raced across the glass. Then it collapsed in a shower of sparkling shards.

I flung the door open and threw myself out on to the track. I tumbled over into the shallow ditch that ran along beside the track and lay there for a few moments, while Eric's car trundled along the track until it veered off into the ditch and came to a dead stop.

My breathing was fast from the shock of it. My chest was heaving. Sweat ran into my eyes. I wiped it away with the back of my hand, and lay still, listening.

Nothing happened. I could hear gulls squawking and the murmur of the sea, but not much else. A puff of air started the grass whispering and rustling. I waited, tense. I needed to know where the bullet had come from before I moved.

Then I experienced another shock as I realized the Glock was in the car. I was a dead duck, lying here. I had to move. All the shooter had to do was walk across from where he lay and stick his rifle in my face. I had to reach the car. Here, in this sheltering ditch, I was helpless, and not really safe at all.

There was no time to think about it. I steeled myself, leapt up and began a mad dash to the car, ducking and weaving as I went.

It was the longest twenty yards I had ever run, and probably the fastest. I heard nothing but I felt a couple of bullets sigh past me. I reached the car and dived behind it, and scrambled the passenger side door open. The Glock hadn't moved. It was still under the driver's seat. I pulled it out and rolled away.

The shooter probably guessed what I was doing. I had been so desperate to reach the car. He was now shooting into the car, using bullets heavy enough to pierce the skin of the side panels. I fired a couple of rounds back in his general direction, just to let him know I was armed now, and then pulled well back, using the cover of a patch of gorse bushes.

I felt better with a weapon in my hand. It wasn't much good against a rifle at distance, but he knew and I knew that he couldn't get up close now. He had lost the advantage of surprise.

I began to move in a wide circle, to see if I could get behind him. There wasn't much chance but it was better for me to be moving than lying still doing nothing. The ground was pretty flat but it was rough ground, with plenty of undulations to provide cover for someone prepared to crawl.

I kept going for a few minutes. Then it became a waste of time. One of his bullets hit the petrol tank and brought the scene to an end with an explosion and a sheet of flame.

I grimaced but I was too far away for the explosion to harm me. When it was over I pulled out my mobile and speed-dialled Bill Peart. Then I cancelled the call and phoned Eric first instead.

'Sorry, Eric. I need another car — unless the Land Rover's ready?'

'It is not! Another car? It's going to cost

you,' he said with a heavy sigh.

'It already has — believe me!'

* * *

While I waited for Eric's lad to fetch me another vehicle, and for the police to arrive, I heard the sound of an engine starting up some distance away. I ran up a low mound, and was in time to see a Range Rover bounce across rough ground a few hundred yards away. When it hit the road it took off at speed. I wasn't too worried about it getting away. At least I could relax now.

But only for the moment. Sal would be back. I knew that.

* * *

Bill Peart said, 'They sent me again.'

'Nice to see you, Bill.'

'I'm bloody sick of this!' He glowered at me. 'Why can't you stay out of trouble for five minutes?'

'I thought I had! I'd been out all day. I was arriving home when all this kicked off. You're lucky I'm still alive.'

He thought about that before he started to laugh. 'Instead of having another murder to solve, you mean?'

242

'Very funny.'

He shook his head and said, 'So what happened this time? No, wait! Put the kettle on first.'

We sat around the table and I opened a new jar of coffee, while the uniforms combed the ground outside and went all over what was left of Eric's car, looking for . . .

I had no idea. Bullets, probably. Shell casings. Fingerprints. Footprints? I don't know. I'm not up on crime-scene stuff and modern forensics. I don't have the time, or the inclination, to watch all those TV series.

'It'll have been Sal,' Bill said moodily after he had heard my account of recent events.

I nodded. 'Probably.'

'There's no-one else, is there?'

'Not to my knowledge.'

'Thank Christ for that!'

I ignored the sarcasm.

'Any chance of finding him?' I asked.

'Every chance. We've just not done it yet.'

I thought I was more likely to find Sal than the Cleveland Police were. But I might not live long enough afterwards to tell anyone.

'Whatever happened to crime prevention?' I asked with exasperation. 'All I seem to hear about is crime solving. Picking up the pieces.'

'We're your friends, Frank,' Bill said sternly. 'Probably the only ones you have.'

My phone rang just then, stopping me responding in a way I thought appropriate.

'It's Henry, Frank. I've got something interesting for you.'

'Oh? What's that?'

'I know where McCardle is getting the money from for the takeover.'

'Where?'

'Not over the phone. Come and see me, the sooner the better.'

34

I was surprised to find Kenny Douglas, as well as Henry, waiting for me.

'Kenny has an interest,' Henry explained.

'I want to protect my pension,' Kenny said with a grin. 'How are you, Frank?'

'Surviving,' I told him. 'What's all this about McCardle, Henry?'

I wasn't troubled by Kenny's presence. As far as I was concerned, the more on the anti-PortPlus band wagon, the better.

'I told you he was skint, got cleaned out in Africa?'

'You did, yes.'

Henry nodded. Then he considered. He was enjoying this.

'Come on, Henry! Get on with it.'

'It's a good story,' Kenny cautioned. 'Well worth waiting for.'

I flopped down into a chair. 'I'm listening.'

Henry grinned and started.

'McCardle remained well-connected, of course. He might have been down to his last million . . . '

'I thought you said he was skint?'

'A figure of speech. Relatively skint.

Anyway, he went back to the Gulf, where a lot of his investment capital had always come from. Abu Dhabi, specifically. He has good friends there.'

'I would like friends there,' Kenny confessed. 'I really would.'

'Henry?' I said impatiently.

'In a nutshell, he got the financial backing he wanted from their sovereign wealth fund.'

'That's where they store their spare cash from the oil and gas sales?'

'Something like that. Right. They use their spare cash to buy into investment opportunities around the world. They're all at it, the oil and gas producers. Qatar, Kuwait, Dubai — even Norway. Not only them either. China does the same thing with its earnings from being the world's workshop.'

So this was the answer to the question that had long bothered me. You don't fund big takeovers from the money in your building society savings account. Abu Dhabi, eh?

'How does it work, Henry?'

'Their sovereign wealth fund is split into a number of divisions — property, equities, etcetera. Managers break it down even further, into different parcels. Some of the investment vehicles are very adventurous. Not for them small, safe returns on government bonds. They go for high risk, high profit schemes.

Football clubs, for instance!'

That brought a smile out of all of us.

'Why haven't they thought of Middles-brough?' I wondered.

'Too high a risk even for them!' Kenny said.

'So,' Henry continued, 'McCardle talked to one of his good friends there, a sheik with a bundle of cash to invest, and persuaded him that Teesport was a wonderful opportunity.'

'A port, though?' I pointed out. 'I know there's land as well but, basically, a port?'

'They're into ports,' Kenny said firmly.

'Really? McCardle?'

'Abu Dhabi. They bought the P&O port operation in the US a few years ago.'

Of course! I remembered that now.

'There was a big political fuss over it, wasn't there?'

'There was.' Kenny nodded. 'But, subject to political safeguards and concessions to Congress, the deal went through.'

'So is that where Mike Rogers came from?'

Henry said, 'That's my thinking. He'll have been a P&O man. McCardle is the man with the ideas and the money, but he needed a man with port expertise.'

It was coming together nicely now. The answers to so many questions. This project was a very big deal, especially for McCardle.

His reputation on the line. He was trusted to come up with the goods. And he had. So the money he needed was available. Everything going well — until his brother turned against him. No way could he let that happen.

'You do realize,' I said slowly, 'that this is why James Campbell was shot and dumped in the sea?'

Kenny said, 'I wondered about that.'

Henry just looked at me.

'Killed,' I said, 'because he had turned against the project. McCardle couldn't have that. Too much was at stake.'

'Then it went wrong,' Henry said, pushing his glasses further up the bridge of his nose with one finger.

I nodded. 'It did. Campbell's body didn't disappear.'

We knew the whole thing now. The picture was clear.

'Well done, Henry!' I said. 'You've got to the bottom of it.'

Henry shrugged modestly. 'Have I?' he said.

'Now we have to think about what to do next. How are we going to stop them?'

I looked round in anticipation.

Henry said, 'How about a coffee?'

★ ★ ★

'What we need to do,' I said over coffee, 'is to find a way of making McCardle's funding disappear. How can we get Abu Dhabi to put its money back in the petty cash box?'

'We?' Henry said.

'All right, all right! I'll do it myself, then.'

Henry was right to object. He couldn't expose himself to the kind of trouble I had encountered. He wouldn't last five minutes if he did.

'Just so's you know,' Henry said.

'I understand. You're a background guy, the man with the brains. Not like me.'

'And I'm too old,' Kenny Douglas said with a grin.

I shook my head with disgust. What a pair!

'Bad publicity,' Henry said.

'What?'

'That's what will make Abu Dhabi run for cover. Bad publicity. They don't like it.'

'Associate them in the public mind with some of these shenanigans,' Kenny contributed. 'They can't afford to be seen in a bad light.'

I nodded. It made sense.

'PortPlus have not said where the money is coming from,' Henry pointed out. 'So ask the question publicly. Insist on it. Get as much as possible out in the open. And then put it alongside questions about the death of James

Campbell. See what happens.'

'Get your head blown off?' Kenny suggested.

'Oh, I'm a candidate for that already!' I told him.

I thought about it. PortPlus wouldn't be the only outfit that didn't appreciate an approach like that. The politicians wouldn't either. Nor would the Chief Constable — not to mention Bill Peart!

35

Nancy was intrigued; intrigued and incensed.

'So that's where the money's coming from! Maybe James knew?'

'I'm sure he did. But so what? Sovereign wealth funds are legitimate investors.'

'Not if they're behaving immorally!'

I shrugged. I wasn't getting into that. Money, especially big money, seldom behaves with moral purpose from what I can see. Profit is the driver, preferably profit free from legal complications. It always has been. We had to be realistic.

'What I'm thinking,' I told her, 'is that we need to go public with what we have against PortPlus, and then link it with Abu Dhabi. Henry's view — and I think he's right — is that the fund managers will shy away from bad publicity. They can't afford it.'

'So they'll dump McCardle?'

'Let's hope so.' I grinned. 'You really are bloodthirsty!'

★ ★ ★

We got to work and sketched out a report that identified all the concerns about the PortPlus project, having first acknowledged that some saw it as an engine of economic recovery and transformation.

Teesport already operated successfully, we argued. Was a takeover going to make it more efficient? Or was it to be, as some feared, an asset stripping exercise that aimed to take value out of land for housing and then pull out?

Then there was the threat to the fishermen's huts at the South Gare to consider, and the future of the seals and other wildlife. The long-term future of the steelworks came into it. And the concern that another nuclear power station would be built, this one right next to Redcar.

We paused to consider.

'It's not enough, is it?' Nancy said.

I shook my head. It wasn't. Yet. We had to do better than this.

'Now we bring James into it,' I said. 'The much-loved, and much-respected, local MP. Half-brother to Donovan McCardle, the Chairman of PortPlus. Initially, James encouraged PortPlus, and supported them. Then he realized there was more to it than he had thought. He had made a mistake. Overall, the project was not in the area's interest. He changed his mind, and prepared to campaign against it. At that point he was murdered, and his body tossed into the sea. Coincidence, or what?'

'And now,' Nancy added, picking up the threads, 'we find that PortPlus have not been open and transparent with local people and their political representatives. We have learned that PortPlus are funded by Abu Dhabi money. Can a Gulf state have Redcar's best interests at heart? Questions about James Campbell's murder must be asked — and answered.'

'That's better,' I said with satisfaction. 'It's coming together nicely now.'

I typed another couple of paragraphs.

'On the face of it, such a huge investment project is very attractive. Yes, there will be concerns and some losses, but the price may be thought worth paying. However, motive has to come into it, too, when our political representatives sit down to take decisions. Genuine investment, or a rip-off for short-term gains? And we have to know where the money is coming from. Greater transparency is needed. Above all, was James Campbell — a serving Member of Parliament — murdered because he was prepared to speak out against the project?'

'And you,' Nancy urged. 'Your role in this. Mention that, too.'

I nodded. She was right. Why not?

So we added a bit about me, about the well-known, local private investigator who had happened upon James Campbell's body, and who ever since had been pursued by thugs and hitmen. Cleveland Police were working night and day . . .

I stopped and mulled it over. It wasn't bad, as a first draft. Polished well, this would put some uncomfortable questions into the public domain and generate no end of horrific publicity for the project and its sponsors. Michael Donnelly and Bill Peart's boss would be livid, and frantic in their efforts to contain the damage.

And the Abu Dhabi sponsors? We'd have to wait and see how they reacted.

'What are your writing skills like?' I asked, turning to Nancy.

★ ★ ★

They weren't bad. Better than mine anyway. While she beavered away over the report, I made contact again with the main Teesside newspaper. This time I kept clear of their business editor, the man who had not been prepared to listen to a word against PortPlus. Instead, I contacted the crime editor. He was interested. I arranged to meet him.

I also spoke to Jack Gregory.

'How's it going, Frank?'

'I've been making waves, Jack, helped by Nancy Peters. James would have been proud of us both.'

'Tell me more.'

'Not over the phone. It's complicated.'

And insecure, I reminded him.

'Can we meet?' he asked.

'As soon as possible.'

★   ★   ★

First I met the *Gazette* crime editor, Jim Edwards, in a Middlesbrough Starbucks not far from Jac Picknett's gallery. I handed over the report Nancy had fine-tuned. He took it and began to speed-read.

'You write this?' he asked when he was done.

I shook my head. 'An associate wrote it.'

'Does she want a job?'

'*She?*'

He grinned. 'Don't tell me it was a man? All that righteous indignation?'

I smiled. 'It shows, does it? You're right. We worked on the draft together. But she did the writing. She's someone who was close to James Campbell.'

'It's good.'

He picked up his coffee mug, and seemed surprised to find it empty. He stared down at the half-dozen pages that I had stapled together, collecting his thoughts.

'This is a big story,' he said eventually, 'easily the biggest that has ever come my way, to be honest. The question is: what to do with it?'

'Print it!'

He shook his head. 'It's not that simple. There are editors, lawyers and owners above me who might well want to suppress it for all sorts of reasons. We're cautious folk in the provincial press, you know.'

I shook my head impatiently. 'Publish and be damned!'

'That old line, eh?' he said with a chuckle.

Then he sighed and his expression changed to serious. 'You've got a lot of balls, Frank, taking this on. Do you know how many big guns you're up against?'

'I've met some of them,' I said, nodding, 'and I've also had to put up with people trying to kill me.'

'So I gather.' He frowned. 'I couldn't print this story as it stands. I'd like to, but I couldn't get away with it.'

'Thanks for the coffee,' I said, pushing back my chair.

'No, wait! I'm not saying no. Far from it.

I'm thinking tactics. What I would like to do is leak this report to someone I know who will put it on the web, and then make sure that a hundred million people around the world know about it in double-quick time.

'Once it's there, I'll go to print. It would be irresponsible and professionally inept not to. I'll do a big piece about this huge story that's sweeping the web, and I'll demand that the authorities investigate and hold back from taking planning decisions relating to the PortPlus project.' He paused and gave me a quizzical look. 'What do you think? Could you go along with that?'

I grinned. 'It's perfect!'

'You're hoping what? That McCardle will lose his funding?'

I shook my head. 'More than that, Jim. I want the murder of James Campbell solved, and his killers punished.'

'This should do it,' Jim Edwards said confidently.

I told Jack Gregory what Nancy and I had discovered, and what had been agreed with the man from the *Gazette*.

He shook his head with astonishment. 'Christ, Frank, you have been busy!'

'Trying to save my own skin, mostly.'

'So James was right about PortPlus? They really are a bunch of charlatans?'

'Worse than that. The phrase 'organized crime' comes to mind. But I'm not too bothered about whether their project is good or not. I want to see them pinned down for Campbell's murder, and for their attempts to send me and Nancy the same way.'

'Quite.'

'So this story is going to break soon.'

'And go viral fast, I would think.'

'I hope so. What I was wondering was if you know a friendly MP, a friend of James perhaps, who could be alerted and prompted to ask questions in Parliament about the whole affair. Demand an investigation, etcetera.'

'Dennis O'Shea would do it. No question.'

'The Middlesbrough MP?'

'Yes. He is — he was — James's closest colleague.'

'Will he do it?'

Jack grinned. 'When I show him this report of yours, he'll jump at it! This could make his career.'

I gave him a copy of our report and left him to it. My feeling was that Nancy and I had done a good day's work. Now we would have to wait for others to do the same.

36

It was a relief to get home after all that. I felt like I had really been through the wringer. Talking, talking, talking all day long. One set of negotiations after another. Not my game. If I was a people person I wouldn't be living somewhere like Risky Point.

Then the phone rang.

'They've gone, Frank. They've bloody gone!'

'Steady, Nancy! What's gone?'

'The pictures! I went back to the house, and somebody's taken them.'

She was struggling to be coherent. She was in a rage.

'Why did you go there again?'

'For the pictures. I told you. James promised me them.'

'Well . . . '

I was thinking her claim to ownership was a bit flimsy. Unless Campbell had actually written something down, it was hard to see the legal process giving Nancy's claim any credibility. In any case, they were worthless.

'Nancy, I know the pictures mean a lot to you. They must have great sentimental value, but they're not actually worth anything. They . . . '

'Don't be stupid, Frank! They're Turners. They're worth an absolute bloody fortune!'

'Nancy, a friend told me . . . '

'I know exactly who's taken them, as well. McCardle! And he's not getting away with it.'

The phone went dead. I looked at it and shook my head before I put it down. I might as well have saved my breath. Nancy was outraged and in full-power mode.

★ ★ ★

While I microwaved some chilli from the freezer, I opened a bottle of an unknown German lager I'd bought from Lidl as an experiment. Or was it Aldi? One or the other. They both offered good deals. The brands were unfamiliar to me but I hadn't had a poor beer yet from them, and they were cheap.

I was doing things mechanically, by habit. My mind was elsewhere. That Nancy! She was certainly something.

Much as I liked her, I had always suspected she knew more than she was telling me. Now here was proof. She had pretended the paintings were of no account, while all the time she had believed them to be priceless. I just couldn't trust her.

I smiled ruefully. But how could I blame her? Getting her hands on genuine Turners would have transformed her life. She could have bought an oligarch-style cruiser as well as a decent house, never mind replace her grandad's old duffel coat!

Then I wondered again where Jac Picknett had seen the pictures. Who had shown her them? The thought that it might have been Nancy brought a little edge to the situation. But surely not? It couldn't have been. But if not Nancy, who? Surely she hadn't known James Campbell?

I reached for the phone.

★ ★ ★

'Oh, hello Frank! I was just thinking about you.'

I smiled. Thinking about me?

'That's nice, Jac. I like the idea of people thinking about me.'

She chuckled.

'Jac, I'm still interested in those pictures I emailed you about. I was wondering where you had seen them previously.'

'Well, that's just it.' She hesitated and then added, 'That's why I was thinking of you.'

'Oh?'

'My friend showed me them. But, oddly, I

can't get in touch with him now. I'm worried about him.'

Alarm bells went off in my head. Suddenly things began to look different. American, eh?

'This friend, Jac. Did he say where he got them?'

'Family heirlooms, he said. Why?'

Was this the time to tell her they weren't his? Probably not. I didn't want her slamming the phone down on me.

'I just wondered,' I told her. 'That's the same story someone else told me.'

I ended the call while she was trying to question me. I wasn't ready to answer questions; I was intent on asking them.

I turned to the computer and switched on. Then I began searching. It didn't take long. The PortPlus story was beginning to break all over the place. Not on the BBC website yet, but they would soon have to pick it up. Our report really was going viral. So was a lot of pleasingly outraged comment.

I couldn't believe how fast Jim Edwards had got to work. Mind you, he had admitted it was the biggest story ever to cross his desk. So he'd had every incentive to go for it.

Whoever his web contact was, he was a good man too. In just a few hours he had plastered it all over the place. Facebook and Twitter were going crazy with comments.

Questions were being asked, opinions offered. The charges and allegations were multiplying. Our report had kicked off a storm.

I switched back to my email inbox. Jim had sent a copy of his piece for the morning edition of the *Gazette*. It was brief, and to the point. Urgent questions were being asked online about the murder of Redcar MP James Campbell, and about the possibility of it being linked to a major investment project that he had opposed.

Jim had also sent me a copy of his article for the lunch time edition of the paper. It was an expanded version of his first piece, concentrating on the spread of the story across the web. A third article was for the evening edition. This was full-on. It set out the case against PortPlus in detail and insisted that there had to be an investigation to determine if the allegations were true.

He had really gone to town. I was hugging myself with satisfaction. This was all, and more, that we had hoped for. I could scarcely believe it was happening so fast.

Then an email from Jack Gregory came into my inbox. Dennis O'Shea had tabled a question on PortPlus, linking it to Campbell's murder, for Prime Minister's Questions in the House of Commons the next day. Even better!

Back to the internet. A couple of hours later, a small item edged onto the BBC website. Abu Dhabi Investments had issued a press release saying they were surprised to be linked to the controversy that had arisen on Teesside. It was most unfortunate. The authority was considering its position and would issue a more detailed statement later.

Bingo!

I rang Henry and asked if he'd seen it.

'Yeah. I've seen it.'

'What do you think? Does it mean what I hope it means?'

He chuckled. 'Too early to celebrate properly, Frank. Better to leave it till tomorrow. But, yes. It probably means they're going to pull out. They have no option.'

'Great!'

'Maybe. But watch yourself, Frank. There'll be some very angry people out there. Don't go on TV, or anything like that. In fact, I would consider going into hiding if I were you.'

*　*　*

It was very hard to think of sleep that night. I kept checking the internet, and watching our story spread. It was all over the world — in just a few hours!

I rang Nancy a couple of times, wanting to

update her and to tell her not to spend time worrying about the fake Turners. But her phone was switched off, or otherwise not working. After the fourth try I began to feel uneasy, worried even. What was it she'd said? She knew who had taken the pictures. And they were not going to get away with it.

What did that mean?

With a sinking feeling, I realized what it might mean: she had gone to try to get them back. To Sutton Castle, in other words. I grimaced, and hoped to God she hadn't.

I monitored the internet, switching between sites, following the story as it exploded across the globe. Plenty of noise now out of the Middle East. Abu Dhabi was not as popular as it would like to be, it seemed. I waited for a more definitive statement from them.

Also, I watched the clock and worked the phone, and fretted. Nancy remained unobtainable.

★   ★   ★

At 1.15 my phone trilled. I grabbed it, hoping it was Nancy. It wasn't.

'Jim Henderson here, Frank.'

'Working late?'

'Only a little later than usual. Did you see the pieces I sent you?'

'I did. Thanks. They're great!'

'We've got momentum with the story, Frank. The internet's going wild.'

'I know. I've seen it. Terrific!'

'I thought I'd let you know things are moving even faster than I had dared hope. A statement came out of Abu Dhabi quarter of an hour ago that I've been waiting for.'

'What did it say?'

'They deny the rumours — as they put it — that Abu Dhabi money is behind the Teesport takeover bid.'

'Does that mean what I hope it means?'

'It means they've pulled the plug. The heat was getting too intense. They have too much to lose around the world to risk their reputation as an honest investor. They're out of it.'

'So McCardle's hung out to dry?'

'It looks that way. And so is PortPlus. It's over. My business editor colleague is going to go nuts in the morning.'

'As are one or two politicians!' I suggested with a broad smile. 'Thanks again, Jim. Oh, by the way, I'm told Dennis O'Shea is going to ask a question in the House tomorrow. He's going to demand a full inquiry.'

'Is he now?' Jim Henderson chuckled. 'Sounds like you've been doing more than just lobbying me.'

'You're right. I want James Campbell's killer, or killers, brought to justice.'

'Me, too. But I'm going home now. Good night, Frank.'

'You, too.'

★ ★ ★

While I was still wondering what to do, the phone went off yet again. It was Bill Peart this time.

'You're still up, Bill?'

'Damn right I am! If only you'd minded your own business, like I told you to do, I could be safe at home in bed now. Instead . . . Guess what?'

'You've got me there,' I said warily. 'What?'

'We're going to arrest your buddies at PortPlus.'

'For what?' I asked, hardly daring to believe it.

'Murder, and attempted murder, to start with. Once they're in the cage we'll see.'

'And you're involved, obviously?'

'I'm preparing the paperwork now. We'll be out at Sutton Castle by dawn. You might want to keep clear — just in case it ever crossed your mind to go sightseeing.'

'Thanks, Bill. I take it you got a breakthrough?'

'Yep. The Geordies squealed. Said they weren't taking a murder rap for the likes of Rogers and McCardle.'

'So they do have some brains between them?'

'Just a few.'

37

I heard a car nudging along the track. What now?

I opened the door and went outside to meet it. Surprisingly, it was daylight already, at least light enough to see without headlights. I shielded my eyes against the twin beams and peered at the approaching car. It wasn't one that was familiar. A BMW, it looked like.

The car stopped. The passenger door swung open. Out stepped Nancy.

'Morning, Frank!'

I gaped. I couldn't believe it.

'Nancy! I've been trying to ring you all night.'

'Oh, I know!' She opened the rear door and reached inside.

'I've got them,' she said, straightening up and turning back to me. 'Look!'

She held up one of the pictures.

By then, another woman had got out of the driver's side. She wore a baseball cap and a denim jacket. I didn't know her.

'Where have you been?' I demanded of Nancy. 'Don't tell me. Not Sutton Castle?'

'Of course,' she said, advancing on me with a beaming smile.

'You might have been killed,' I said lamely. 'And you went there for these damned pictures?'

'I wanted them. James promised me them!'

'And McCardle just abandoned these priceless Turners? Handed them over, just like that?'

'Oh, I know!' She shrugged ruefully. 'You were probably right, and they're not Turners. Otherwise my dear stepbrother wouldn't have abandoned them. After all, he was prepared to have me killed to stop me claiming them. That's why he had people looking for me. But I still wanted them anyway, even if they aren't valuable, because they belonged to James.'

'McCardle abandoned them? What happened? He just handed them over?'

'McCardle wasn't there. He'd cleared out, along with that Rogers guy.'

'They've left?'

She nodded.

Then I took a step backwards. I had almost missed it. When things are unbelievable, it's easy to do.

'What did you just say?' I said slowly. 'Your stepbrother?'

'Yes, that's right.'

She thrust the picture she was holding into my hands and returned to the car for the others. The woman with the baseball cap stood on the far side of the car, silently observing this little tableau, not offering to help. I wondered who she was.

'Nancy, you do realize what you're saying?' I demanded. 'After all we've been through, you're telling me now that Donovan McCardle is your stepbrother?'

'He's a lot older than me,' she said with a shrug. 'I never knew him at all.'

'What about James?' I asked faintly. 'What was he?'

'Another one,' she said succinctly, holding the second fake Turner at arms' length to admire.

'Also your stepbrother?'

'Yes. The two of them came with Mum when she married my dad. Then she had me.'

'Quite a family!'

'What?' She glanced at me. 'Oh, I see. Yes, James and Donovan hated one another.'

'What about you?'

'Simple, really. I loved James. He was a real brother to me, not just a half-brother. Donovan? I'd never even met him until recently.'

I was reeling by then. I put the picture I was holding down on the steps and swore at her. She seemed genuinely surprised, shocked even.

'You don't think I had a right to know this?' I demanded.

'What difference does it make?' she asked, again genuinely surprised.

I just shook my head.

'Anyway, who's this?' I asked, looking at the woman in the baseball cap.

'She works there, at Sutton Castle. At least, she did. Her job's gone now. But she kindly offered to run me here. Maybe she'll get to keep the car. I don't know.'

Nancy was too preoccupied with her bloody pictures to be interested in telling me any more. I shook my head again and pulled out my mobile to call Bill Peart.

'News for you, Bill. McCardle and Rogers have pulled out. They've abandoned Sutton Castle.'

'How do you know that?' he asked suspiciously.

'Trust me! They've gone. The place is wide open.'

'Do you happen to know where they've gone, by any chance?'

'Nope. But my guess would be an airport somewhere nearby, probably a private one. They need to put themselves out of reach quickly.'

The phone went dead. He didn't even thank me for the tip-off.

'There's gratitude for you,' I murmured.

But I was smiling. I wouldn't want to be

anywhere near Bill now he had this to deal with.

★ ★ ★

'So what's happening, Frank?'

For the first time, Nancy displayed interest in something other than her damned pictures.

'PortPlus is finished,' I told her. 'Abu Dhabi have been frightened off by the negative publicity. They've pulled out. So McCardle's takeover is dead in the water, and the police are on their way to arrest him for murder.'

She shrieked with delight.

I grinned and said, 'So you are still interested?'

'Oh, yes!' she assured me. 'That's all I ever wanted.'

That and the bloody pictures, of course!

Although things had gone well that night in a strategic sense, I was feeling out of sorts. Bloody Nancy! I had known I couldn't trust her. Of course I had. She had never actually lied to me, not that I knew of, but getting information out of her had always been like pulling teeth.

She had told me what she wanted me to know, not what I had wanted to know. All along, that had been true. I had been enlisted to help her bring down McCardle and avenge James. Her strategy had worked. But I resented the fact that we had never really been partners, not in the fullest sense. I felt used. It wasn't a good feeling.

So I picked up my jacket and announced that I was heading for the beach. I needed to clear my head. Nancy nodded and returned to appreciating her pictures.

The driver fell in beside me as I passed through the gate. 'Mind some company?' she asked.

'Not at all,' I said without much interest. 'I'm Frank Doy, by the way.'

'Yes, I know.'

'Thanks for giving Nancy a lift.'

'You're welcome.'

She was tall and slim, and nearly as tall as me. American, too, I realized. Probably came with Rogers.

'So your job is over?' I said as we walked towards the top of the path.

'Not quite,' she said.

Thankfully, she seemed as uninterested in conversation as I was. That suited me.

'Frank!' I heard Nancy call.

We were at the top of the path by then. I stopped and looked back.

'Are you taking Sal with you?'

It took a moment, but the penny did drop.

Scarcely trusting my voice to perform, I said over my shoulder, 'That's you, presumably?'

The woman beside me nodded. 'That's me.'

'Yes!' I called to Nancy.

Then we resumed our walk, with me thinking fast. I wasn't armed. I was certain Sal would be. Where would she make her move?

That was obvious. There was only one place it could be, and I was taking her right to it. All her dreams come true. Well, let it come. I was ready, thanks to Nancy.

My pulse was racing. My brain was scanning the options, and simultaneously watching for signals.

I considered moving first, and simply grabbing and overpowering her, but for all I knew the gun was already in her hand, her finger on the trigger. I needed to know. Until we got to the place, I had time to find out.

I paused to gaze out to sea. 'So beautiful here,' I murmured, 'especially in the early morning.'

'It is,' she said.

She was fidgeting a bit, eager to get on with it. She didn't like the pause.

I moved on a few paces, and stopped again. We were close to the spot now. An Olympic long-jumper could have made it in one bound from where we stood.

I moved close to her and tensed, ready to unleash when she made her move. But I still spoke to her calmly, in a relaxed way. Nothing had to show.

'This path is very treacherous,' I said, 'especially when it's wet. So keep close. I know where the problems are.'

I guessed her reflexes would be faster than mine. It went with her trade. If she saw anything she didn't like, the gun would be out faster than I could stop it. I had to let her feel in charge, and wait my chance.

'Wasn't there an accident around here recently?' she asked.

I nodded. 'There was. A man fell from the path.'

'Where from?'

'Just over there,' I said, pointing ahead a few paces.

She made her move.

Her gun arm started to lift from her side.

Because I was pointing past her, my own arm was already raised. I swept it down now, fast and hard.

I grabbed her wrist and pointed the gun downwards. She turned and threw me over her hip, but I kept my grip on her wrist. Then we were on the ground, writhing at one another. Fingernails raked my face. I crashed an elbow into her face and head-butted her. The gun came loose. I kicked it aside, and over the edge.

Somehow she got loose and sprang to her feet. A knife appeared. She was bleeding heavily from the face. We faced each other.

'Give it up!' I panted. 'You're not going to win now.'

She snarled and sprang at me, the knife blade catching the early morning light. I jumped and kicked out with both feet, catching her heavily. She staggered backwards. I landed flat on my back, winded.

It was the same thing, the same as with her partner. When I got back up she was gone. Not quite from the same place, but near enough.

I glanced over the edge. For a moment I thought I saw something in the water, between two big rocks. But only for a moment. Then it was gone.

Justice for James, I thought grimly as I straightened up, catching my breath. Whichever of them had pulled the trigger, they had both gone the same way as him in the end.

38

'We got them,' Bill said. 'They were on a private jet at Teesside Airport, waiting to take off.'

'You arrested them?' Jac asked.

He nodded.

'Well done!'

'All in a day's work,' he said modestly.

'Unfortunately,' Nancy said, 'they won't get what they deserve, even if he is my step-brother. Nothing will bring James back.'

'Indeed,' Jac said.

Bill looked grave.

I felt my house had become too crowded.

'About those pictures?' Jac said to Nancy.

'Oh, yes! Let's look at them again.'

They were big buddies now, those two. Jac had turned up later the day Sal fell to her death, looking for news of her new friend, Mike Rogers. She had taken the news in her stride, especially when she learned that Nancy had acquired the pictures.

Now the Grimshaw had their joint attention. It was the one painting Nancy wasn't very keen on, and the only one of the three that interested Jac. It was also the only one worth anything. Maybe £200,000, according to Jac. Enough to allow Nancy to get her boat fixed and buy a proper house, and the commission in prospect was enough to make Jac's eyes gleam. I left them to it.

★ ★ ★

I strolled over to the edge of the cliff to listen to the sea and the gulls. Jimmy Mack joined me after a few minutes. We stood together in silence. It was a relief.

'A bad business,' Jimmy said eventually, nodding towards the path to the beach.

'Yep.'

'I used to wonder how this place got its name.'

'It must always have been risky here?' I suggested.

'Only for some,' he said. 'It's suited me well enough.'

'And me,' I admitted, turning away and giving him a grin. 'Don't worry about me!'

We watched Bill Peart trudge across to join us.

'Your women!' he said to me, shaking his head.

'My women?'

'They were getting on so well together, too.'

'What's happened now?'

'They can't agree on the percentage rate Jac should get as commission on selling that bloody picture!'

'They're business people, you see,' Jimmy Mack said philosophically. 'It runs in both families.'

'Women, eh?' Bill said to me, almost sympathetically. 'When will you learn?'

'That's what I keep asking him,' Jimmy Mack said.

'What can I tell you?' I asked, grinning. 'Maybe when I get to your age . . . '

* * *

Later, Bill took me aside.

'You did really well, Frank. You've achieved incredible things.'

He chuckled and added, 'The politicians and my chief constable are queuing up to go on television and say how they always knew PortPlus were a bunch of crooks! Only yesterday they were singing from a different hymn sheet. It's down to you, that.'

'Not only me, Bill. I had a lot of help.'

'You mostly, then,' he amended.

'Then there was this,' he said, nodding to the path that led down to the beach. 'You all right with this?'

'I suppose so.' I grimaced. 'It was them or me at the time, Bill. If ever it gets to me, I'll just remind myself what they did to James Campbell.'

He nodded with approval. 'And that lot in there?' he asked, gazing over my shoulder towards my house.

'Perhaps you can take the pair of them back to Redcar for me?'

He laughed. 'Too much for you, are they?'

'Just a bit. I'm going to take Jimmy Mack's advice when it comes to women.'

'Oh? What's that?'

'Have nothing to do with them!'

* * *

I was relaxed about it all now. Just glad it was over. But I hadn't told Bill everything I felt. I wasn't much bothered by what had happened on the cliff-top path. That wouldn't cause me sleepless nights. There was a kind of rough justice about that. It was the memory of James Campbell in the water off the end of the breakwater at the South Gare that I suspected would trouble me for a long time to come. Some things you could never have done anything about, but they are still the ones that come back to haunt you in the small hours.

We do hope that you have enjoyed reading this large print book.

Did you know that all of our titles are available for purchase?

We publish a wide range of high quality large print books including:
Romances, Mysteries, Classics
General Fiction
Non Fiction and Westerns

Special interest titles available in large print are:
The Little Oxford Dictionary
Music Book
Song Book
Hymn Book
Service Book

Also available from us courtesy of Oxford University Press:
Young Readers' Dictionary
(large print edition)
Young Readers' Thesaurus
(large print edition)

For further information or a free brochure, please contact us at:
Ulverscroft Large Print Books Ltd.,
The Green, Bradgate Road, Anstey,
Leicester, LE7 7FU, England.
Tel: **(00 44) 0116 236 4325**
Fax: **(00 44) 0116 234 0205**

Other titles published by Ulverscroft:

RUN FOR HOME

Dan Latus

British counter-intelligence officer Harry Gibson finds the murdered bodies of his three colleagues in their safe houses in Prague and knows he has to get out before he becomes the fourth. The uncertainty of the attacker's identity ensures Harry can trust no one. Seeking sanctuary back in the UK, there is no peace with so many unanswered questions and the knowledge that someone dear to him has been left behind. Harry must return to Prague and submerse himself in the changing and dangerous landscape if he is to uncover the far-reaching conspiracy in the ranks of his own service.

OUT OF THE NIGHT

Dan Latus

One headless body, on the beach near Frank Doy's home on the Cleveland coast, was regrettable, two more were disturbing. But when an uncommunicative woman arrives at his house in the dead of night, only to disappear again, Doy is involved in something worrying. His search for her uncovers a mysterious man with a private art collection and some Russian emigres. Led deeper into the strange events occurring in Port Holland and nearby Meridion House, Frank tries to unearth the secrets surrounding him and save the life of his desperate female visitor . . .

RISKY MISSION

Dan Latus

A mysterious young woman offers Frank Doy good money to drive her to a secret location in central Europe. And despite being warned off by her husband, Harry George — a dangerous Teesside gangster — Frank agrees to her request. But it's risky and the risks soon multiply. Mrs George is also taking along her two young children and a million pounds and Frank still has no idea where they are going. Meanwhile, Harry George wants — *needs* — his money back. But there's someone far more dangerous from his wife's past, who also has an interest in the money, and more . . .

NEVER LOOK BACK

Dan Latus

Living quietly in Northumberland, ex-spook Jake Ord is awakened early one morning by a sniper's bullets that only narrowly miss. It seems his old life has caught up with him. In the nearby village, MI5 agent Anna Mason catches his eye — she's on duty, but she won't reveal why . . . yet. Then as Jake thwarts an ambush, he decides he needs help and he summons Dixie, an ex-colleague and best friend of his late wife Ellie. Together, with Anna's help, they unravel an assassination plot that has political implications and confront the man they hold responsible for Ellie's untimely death.

SNOW WASTED

Matthew Malekos

Forensic pathologist Dr Karen Laos is approached by the Ministry of Defence and dispatched as a civilian contractor to Cyprus. A soldier stationed on the island has been murdered, the crime bearing similarities to the killing of another serviceman the previous year. The Foreign Office insists on a British citizen performing the autopsy, whilst hoping that Laos's own Greek-Cypriot ancestry will placate the local police force. Against the beautiful backdrop of a Mediterranean summer, an undercurrent of vice and deceit simmers, and Laos must work against the odds to restore law and order.

RANDOM TARGETS

James Raven

A sniper launches a series of deadly attacks on Britain's motorways, striking during rush hour and causing total carnage. No one knows who he is, or why he's doing it — and as the death toll rises, fear grips the nation. It's up to DCI Jeff Temple of the Major Investigations department to bring the killing spree to an end — but, as he closes in on the sniper, Temple makes a shocking discovery about the motive behind the attacks. A ghastly precedent has been set, and Temple realizes that any motorway driver risks becoming a random target . . .